The Last Crimes of Peregrine Hind

SIERRA SIMONE

NO BIRD PRESS

One

PEREGRINE

1710

THE ROAD WAS a ribbon of horseshit over the purple moor.

Peregrine Hind sat atop his horse at the crest of a cragged Devonshire hill, staring at the distant gleam of Far Hope nestled into its valley. He couldn't imagine the number of candles it took to light the Dartham family seat, but he also wasn't surprised by the sheer waste of it all. The Darthams were like that—careless and prodigal.

But tonight they would pay for it, and ironically enough, it would be their own extravagance that would undo them. It was the week before the annual Michaelmas ball, which was why the manor house was glowing so merrily into the dark. It was also why the road was covered in horseshit, which had accumulated under the constant traffic of visitors coming from everywhere across the kingdom. In any other circumstance, so many coaches creaking their way through this wild and lonely landscape would be like a river of gold to a highwayman like Peregrine Hind.

But he only cared about one coach tonight.

With a soft cluck, he turned his horse back east to where the road from Exeter dipped into a steep, wooded valley. His friends were waiting at the bottom, their mounts already hidden deep in the trees.

"Well?" Lyd asked as Peregrine came to a stop. She was pacing while the others sat checking their pistols. Her jaw was tight, her normally pale cheeks flushed. "Anything yet?"

"No." Peregrine looked up at the moon through the trees. "The innkeeper did say it would be late."

Peregrine paid innkeepers all around Devonshire to give him information when he needed it. Even the keepers of the finer establishments were susceptible to bribery, so long as they were never connected to any crimes that came of the information given—and Peregrine was careful never to let those connections be known. It served his purposes to be thought unnervingly omniscient, his movements and motives shrouded in mystery.

It had given him the reputation of the most infamous highwayman in England, but after four years of terrorizing the roads, Peregrine could conclusively say that the recipe of infamy was much simpler than people seemed to think:

Half preparation.

Half indifference to death.

Peregrine no longer cared very much if he lived or died—and really, when stealing a mere twelve pence could get someone taken to Tyburn, a highwayman was already a dead thief walking. At thirty-four, Peregrine was already older than most in his profession ever lived to be, but the thought rarely bothered him. He'd come from the war, after all, from the bloody, desperate fighting in the Low Countries, where death stalked every man regardless of age or station. He never thought he'd live this long, had assumed from the moment he signed his name to the rolls of the Queen's army that he wouldn't make it to twenty-five, much less the age he was now. He'd joined the army anyway in order to send his much-needed wages to his mother and siblings, but when he'd returned, he'd found his family and their farm in ruins. Anyone he'd ever loved—any purpose he'd ever had after his career as a soldier—was gone. Dead and cold in the ground.

Now he only drew breath to destroy the Dartham family, and tonight, at long last, that destruction would begin.

"I hope she's with him," Lyd said, her voice shaking a little. "I want to see her face." Lyd had her own reasons for hating the Darthams—and the duchess in particular.

"The innkeeper said she would be with him," Peregrine replied, staring at where the road broke through the trees at the top of the hill. They would wait for the coach to work its halting way to the bottom and then begin its ascent up the other side. That way, they could free the horses without worrying about a rolling coach injuring them. Peregrine didn't hurt horses—or people—if he could help it, and he usually could. While he paid his army of innkeepers to spread stories of his bloody cruelty, he had no interest in dealing pain or death these days.

He couldn't even shake the nightmares from the war he'd left four years ago.

And what did I get for those nightmares? Peregrine asked himself as he watched a cloud drift over the moon. *What did I get for killing all those strangers for some other stranger's crown?* A dead family and a farm that had been enclosed for the Duke of Jarrell's sheep.

Which was why tonight, he'd make an exception to his usual rule about hurting or killing; why tonight, he'd embrace whatever nightmares may come. Because tonight, he was going to kill the Duke of Jarrell. Peregrine was going to kill him in the chilly, lonesome dark, the same dark in which Peregrine's pregnant sister had died as she'd waited outside of Far Hope's doors for help. Help that never came.

A distant creak and clack announced an approaching coach. The rest of the band—three thieves plus Lyd—got to their feet.

"Last chance to leave," Peregrine told them. They were brave, but the murder of a duke and the robbery of a duchess was a Rubicon. They'd be wanted criminals forever; they would be given a more vicious death than the usual Tyburn jig if they were caught. And while Peregrine and Lyd had revenge on their minds, the other thieves were here for money, plain and simple, and there was no telling how much the duke would have with him. It could be enough to set them up for life, or it might only be enough to buy them a pair of secondhand boots.

But even knowing that, none of them left. With nods at Peregrine, they melted into the trees near the spot where he'd confront the coach, ready to swarm the conveyance and disarm any guards or passengers. Peregrine urged his own horse up and into the trees too, deep enough that he was hidden from moonlight, but only a few seconds away from the road itself.

Then they waited.

As he'd known it would, the coach made its way slowly down the hill, using blocks under the wheels to temper its descent. As it came closer, the moonlight gleamed along its ornate trim and illuminated an image painted on the outside of its door: two stags framing a shield, which was adorned with a sun and moon and topped with a single golden key.

The Dartham family crest.

The coach made it safely to the bottom of the hill, and then the two footmen stowed the blocks and walked alongside the coach as the horses began to pull it up the hill. Peregrine's friends would take care of the footmen; his role would be to stop the coach's progress and prevent the driver from arming himself.

Flooded with a grim sort of excitement, he pressed in with his calves and surged forward on his mount, breaking through the trees and charging in front of the coach.

"Stand and deliver!" Peregrine cried.

All hell broke loose.

The Dartham horses shied—the driver lurched as if to reach for a gun—the coach came to an ungainly stop as the footmen raced to the door, almost certainly to arm themselves with a gun stashed inside. The thieves slipped out from their hiding places, and Lyd dissuaded the coachman from any heroics with a pistol aimed steadily at his heart.

Peregrine was already off his horse, and as his thieves subdued the two footmen, he flung open the door to the carriage and lunged inside, knowing that brashness and speed would be his only defense if the duke was armed.

It was dark inside the cabin, and before he saw the single occupant scrambling for the opposite door, he detected an oddly lovely scent.

Like cloves and orange peels, maybe. Like Christmas.

Then he saw the duke, and all other observations left his mind. He seized the murderer of his family by his coat and hauled him bodily out of the coach, sending him sprawling onto the damp dirt of the road.

Peregrine hopped easily to the ground and took two long strides over to the duke. "He was alone," he told Lyd, and she swore in response.

Lyd had wanted the duchess. Badly.

The duke was just pushing himself to his hands and knees when Peregrine pressed a boot to his shoulder and shoved the duke back onto his rump. Peregrine then raised his pistol, already loaded and primed.

He was grateful for the bright moon tonight. He hoped the duke would see enough of Peregrine's sister in Peregrine's features to feel thoroughly haunted by his sins as he died. But then the man on the road lifted his terrified face, and Peregrine froze.

Yes, those were the extravagant clothes a Dartham would wear; yes, there was the skin that seemed to shimmer the palest gold. Yes, there were those dark eyes, which Peregrine knew would be a deep sapphire if he peered closely enough. But this was not the duke.

This was not the duke.

Peregrine swore to himself as he studied the man's face, but there could be no doubt. Reginald Dartham had narrow eyes set closely together, a thin mouth, and a scattering of pockmarks across his jaw. But this man had an entirely different look to him: wide eyes fringed with long lashes, a full mouth, and a jaw carved in a fine, unblemished line. And while Reginald was well known for his elaborate periwigs, even while traveling, it was this man's real hair which tumbled darkly around his shoulders as he scrambled to his knees.

It gleamed like silk in the moonlight.

"Stop," Peregrine ordered coldly, his pistol still raised.

The man stopped, his face tilted toward Peregrine. There was no doubt now that Peregrine had gotten a better look. While the duke was in his forties, this man couldn't be more than twenty-five.

"Please," the man breathed. "Please. I have money—there's money in there—"

"We'll be taking that as it is," Peregrine interrupted. "Who are you, and why are you in the Dartham's coach?"

"I'm S-Sandy—Alexander. Alexander Dartham." The

young man swallowed, and then breathed again, "Please. *Please.*"

An unpleasant stab of empathy followed the man's pleas. How often had Peregrine heard those words on a battlefield? Or after the smoke had settled, when all they could do for the wounded was hold them down and hope the surgeon could amputate quickly?

But then Peregrine remembered his sister and the little niece or nephew he never got to meet. He remembered the cold graves of his mother and brother.

Likely they had pleaded too.

Heart once again hardened, he stared down at Alexander Dartham. He'd heard of the duke's younger brother—a notorious rakehell who gambled and swived his way through London. They said no man or woman was safe from his charms, and Peregrine reluctantly admitted to himself that he could see why. Alexander was very beautiful, and on his knees like this . . . also dangerously stirring.

"Where is the duke?" Peregrine demanded, tamping down the flare of heat he felt looking at the brother of his enemy. "He's supposed to be passing through here."

"He took a horse and rode to Far Hope," Alexander said. "This morning. He was worried about being any later than he already was to receive his guests. Please. *Don't.* I can give you anything you want. Anything."

"No, you cannot," Peregrine informed him.

No one could bring back the dead.

One of the thieves relieved Lyd on coachman duty. She climbed down and came to stand next to Peregrine. "You should kill him," she said bluntly. "Hasn't it been your design to destroy them all anyway?"

It had been—although he hadn't intended to *kill* anyone aside from Reginald. After the duke's death, the plan went, he would rob the duke's widow and the new duke of everything that could be carried off, and then he would burn Far Hope to the ground.

And then what, he didn't know. All his careful preparations ended with Far Hope in embers. Maybe he'd retire.

Maybe he'd keep roaming the roads until he was inevitably caught and even more inevitably hanged.

But this was an unexpected difficulty. If he let this younger Dartham live, then Alexander would tell Reginald that he was being sought by a highwayman, not for money, but for murder. Peregrine's opportunities for revenge would shrink further—not to mention that Reginald would no doubt make sure Peregrine was hunted by the law more than he already was.

Which would be...inconvenient.

Peregrine looked back at the young lord, his pistol steady in front of the man's face. He hadn't killed anyone since the war, and even then, the battles had been volleys of smoke and mud and screams, utter chaos, impossible to tell who he'd killed or if his musket had struck anything at all.

Never had he killed someone like this—in stillness and in quiet, with them unarmed and helpless in front of him.

But his sister had died in stillness and in quiet too, she and her unborn child, and Peregrine didn't know what else to live for if it wasn't avenging her death, along with the deaths of his mother and brother. Why not start here?

Why not make Reginald Dartham feel part of what Peregrine had felt when he'd lost his entire family?

He curled his finger around the trigger.

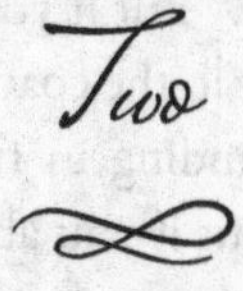

Two

SANDY

"WAIT, WAIT!" Sandy blurted, lifting his hands. His mind raced. He'd been in worse scrapes than this, surely—that time he was caught with a Bohemian princess in his bed came to mind, or perhaps the time a Spanish ambassador realized Sandy had been cheating at cards and was ready to fight a duel over it.

Sandy was very used to people wanting to kill him— honestly, it was starting to become something of a Friday night routine—but never had anyone seemed so emotionless about it. Usually, they were howling with indignation or livid with rage, and all Sandy had to do was remind them that he was the son of a dead duke and the brother of a living one, and then whatever it was went away.

But he'd have to do more than charm his way out of this one, especially if Reginald was involved. He had no doubt that this person had a very good reason for wanting to kill his brother, since Reginald was a miserable shit of a man. Not to mention that he was also a *very wealthy* miserable shit of a man, so his robbery or murder would brand any thief deep into tavern songs and fireside stories forever.

"You can kill me, I promise, you can kill me whenever you like," Sandy said quickly, still thinking of a plan as the words tumbled from his mouth. "But if you kill me here, you'll only get whatever valuables are in the coach."

The highwayman standing in front of him didn't react, and Sandy rushed on. "But if you abduct me instead, you can force my brother to pay any ransom you want, and *then* you can still kill me after you get his money. See? You'll get what you want, plus money! Everyone wins!"

The woman standing next to the highwayman was tall and slender, her long limbs displayed in the breeches and tailored coat she wore. She looked familiar, but Sandy couldn't quite place her, although her voice reminded him of . . . someone.

"He has a point," she said. "But Sandy is slippery. He'll try to escape."

Hmm. She talked about Sandy like she knew him. That probably didn't bode well.

Sandy put his hand over his heart like he was swearing an oath. "I'm not slippery! I won't try to escape!" He was definitely planning on escaping. The first chance he got. "And how do you know me again?" he asked her.

She didn't deign to answer, instead turning toward the highwayman. "We might have to kill him, Peregrine," she said quietly.

Peregrine.

Sandy's blood ran cold—well, colder—and then suddenly and fitfully hot. Peregrine Hind was, depending on whom one asked, either a devil who tortured his victims and then left no survivors, *or* a gallant thief who never hurt his victims or their horses and who gave most of what he robbed to needy families in nearby parishes.

Either way, Sandy was currently at the mercy of a legend,

not a man, and that didn't feel like a safe place to be. Even if Peregrine Hind was a very tall legend. With very powerful thighs. And very broad shoulders.

And pale, eerie eyes that glittered in the moonlight.

"You can still kill me," Sandy volunteered helpfully. "I'll be your captive the whole time. And you'll get a ransom on top of it. And also, it will really, really incense my brother. Like really." Reggie wouldn't mind so much that Sandy had been kidnapped, but he would hate the paying part. Sandy already cost him plenty of money simply by existing. Well, and existing so lavishly, but Reggie could afford it.

Peregrine studied him, his face betraying nothing. In the stories, highwaymen always had masks and wide-brimmed hats. The other thieves had some variation on the uniform, but Peregrine Hind wore none of that. His black hair was tied back in a simple queue like a soldier, and his face was unmasked, revealing dramatic, ivory features: a high forehead, a strong nose, and a grim, sharp-edged mouth. His clothes were simple—dark breeches, dark coat, dark boots—nothing trimmed or fine, even though it all looked clean and of decent quality.

Nothing about him suggested he was a man used to treating himself with the finer things. At that, Sandy's heart sunk a little. Maybe money wasn't an effective lure after all.

Given the lack of mask and hat, and his overall cold, efficient demeanor, Sandy suspected that Peregrine Hind wasn't after melodrama or notoriety either. That meant Sandy could think of only one other reason a man would want to kill his brother, and that was revenge.

Which was not ideal.

He could work with a craving for money or fame—those urges were mollified easily enough. But revenge? He'd seen enough of it at court and in the Second Kingdom to know its bitter effects well. Revenge was a flame that burned without air, a sword that cut without a blade. It listened to nothing but its own counsel, and it had no master but itself.

A man bent on revenge was not a man easily persuaded.

But Sandy had cheated at cards long enough to read infinitesimal cues, and so he didn't miss the quick flick of Peregrine's eyes over to his band of fellow robbers, who had tied the footmen and coachman to a tree and were now standing by the road as they watched Sandy's desperate ploy unfold.

Peregrine cared about them. Or at least cared what they thought.

Sandy shifted his strategy a little, pitching his voice so the others could hear him better.

"The duke wouldn't think twice about paying five thousand pounds," he said loudly. "Maybe more. I'm his heir, you know, and he'd pay anything to get me back."

Sandy was fairly certain that Reggie would have his limit when it came to paying for a brother he despised . . . but the thieves didn't need to know that part. Not when they were casting each other round-eyed looks and mouthing the words *five thousand pounds.*

Peregrine seemed aware of this, aware of every murmur and glance that passed between his friends, though it all happened behind his back. "That's a princely sum, indeed," Peregrine said after a minute.

"I'm a princely man," Sandy replied, but Peregrine didn't smile, didn't respond at all, except to look over his shoulder at his fellow thieves.

"It *is* a lot of money," one of them, a short and stocky man, said. "Even split between us all, it could last the rest of our lives."

The others chimed in with agreements. Peregrine looked to the woman, who stood between him and the other thieves, her pistol still ready in her hand.

"What do you say?"

"That much money would set the duke well on the road to ruin," she said thoughtfully. "And you could still kill Sandy after you got it, if you needed to."

Sandy again. This woman must know him, but how? He mentally flipped through wine-soaked memories of London and Oxford while outwardly he tried to look sweet and pliant and like he'd be a very docile captive.

After a long, breathless moment, Peregrine gave his lieutenant a crisp nod. He shoved the pistol in his belt. "As you say."

"*Thank you*," Sandy breathed. His relief was entirely genuine, no playacting there whatsoever. "I'll be the very best captive, I promise. I even like being tied up!"

That part was also entirely true. He did like being tied up. And he had to say, as disagreeable as it was to be a captive of a man who planned to kill him, the thought of this stern-mouthed legend lashing his wrists together sped Sandy's pulse in a way that had nothing to do with fear.

Or maybe *something* to do with fear, but the fun kind.

"I'll take him to the priory," Peregrine was telling the woman. "Free the horses. Leave the footmen here, and then have Ned ride the coachman to the next bridge. That should put the coachman close enough to Far Hope that the duke can hear of our ransom demand by tomorrow. And tell him that the duke needs to send his response to The Stag's Head in Chagford."

The woman dipped her head to indicate she understood, and then turned away. But not before giving Sandy a small sniff of disapproval.

A sniff he felt a little wounded by, honestly.

"Stand," Peregrine told Sandy, so Sandy stood, taking a moment to mourn his breeches, which now had dirt on the knees, and probably on the arse too. It was bad enough to be almost murdered and now kidnapped, but he was really, really fond of these breeches! They were sensible yet stylish, and he very much doubted the band of roving highwaymen had access to a good laundress.

There was a small sound, and Sandy looked up at the highwayman, who now had an eyebrow lifted the tiniest amount.

"Did you just sigh at me?" Sandy asked.

"We don't have time for you to inventory the state of your clothes," Peregrine said, wrapping a hand around Sandy's upper arm and dragging him up the hill. It was a very big hand, with long fingers and a wide palm. The kind of hand that would splay easily across Sandy's chest or between his shoulder blades while Sandy was being bent over a bed. "We can't risk staying here."

Sandy didn't bother to point out that *he* could risk staying here and encountering another rider or coach who might help him, because he didn't think Peregrine would appreciate the observation. In any event, they were already to Peregrine's horse, where the highwayman was pulling a coil of rope free.

He didn't object as his wrists were bound and the other end of the rope tied to the saddle, or when Peregrine slid his hands inside Sandy's jacket and up his thighs to make sure Sandy was completely unarmed. In fact, Sandy even shivered a little as Peregrine's fingers ran an efficient search along the rims of his shoes, probing the tops of his stocking-clad feet and the knobs of his ankles.

"You missed a spot," Sandy said.

"I don't think so," said the highwayman.

"But you didn't even check the most interesting places," pouted Sandy. "If you untie me, I can show you what they are."

Peregrine Hind's mouth didn't change from its humorless line, but Sandy saw the drop of his eyes, the way his gaze burned from Sandy's mouth to his chest and down to his hips.

Peregrine's hand flexed at his side, and for a moment, Sandy thought his captor was about to touch him again.

But he merely shook his head and mounted his horse. Sandy's rope remained tied to the saddle; he'd have to walk alongside the horse as they went.

"I'll go slowly," Peregrine said as he took the reins. "So long as you behave."

"You'd be the first to make me," said Sandy, but he flashed a big smile to show that he'd be cooperative. He had no wish to fight the highwayman on this, because he was fairly certain he'd lose.

As Peregrine clucked at the horse and they began moving, Sandy could see every flex and press of the expert rider's legs as he rode. He could see the highwayman's strong hands on the reins, casual and powerful all at once.

And with the excellent scenery and the sedate pace, with his hands bound and his body still thrumming with the shaky glee of having just escaped death for a time, Sandy found he didn't mind the walk to the highwayman's lair very much at all.

Three

PEREGRINE

IT WAS ONLY an hour to the priory, but it felt much longer to Peregrine. And that had less to do with his thwarted revenge than it did with the comely captive he had tied to his saddle.

Alexander Dartham's hair spilled everywhere in shimmering waves as he moved, and the moving continually revealed his breeches' superlative tailoring as the fabric clung to his thighs and buttocks when he walked. And whenever he would lag behind the horse and whine that he was tired of walking—which was often—Peregrine would turn around and see a lush pout designed to drive any red-blooded person wild.

By the time they'd gone through a scatter of lonely hills to the narrow seam where the priory sat hidden, Peregrine was at his wit's end. His palms itched to slide over the Dartham heir's sleek thighs; his fingers twitched to tangle themselves in all that soft hair. The scent he'd noticed in the coach was all around him now, spicy and sweet at the same time.

Peregrine's entire body was in riot just from being *near* Alexander Dartham for the length of a ride. How would he bear it when he had Alexander locked away in his hideout for days on end?

But it couldn't be that he was *really* attracted to a scion of the family he loathed, Peregrine reassured himself. It had simply been too long, that was all. During the war, there had been plenty of opportunities to satisfy himself, but being an outlaw in rural Devonshire was a different situation, and he hadn't had the time or luxury to find new lovers. He'd been living more or less like a monk for the last four years—all the more ironic, given his current home.

"I don't want to submit a complaint so early in my captivity," Alexander said as they came to a stop in front of the hideout. "But this is a little déclassé for even my deteriorated taste."

Peregrine looked at the crumbling monastery and imagined how it must look to the brother of a duke. The overgrown entrance was partially blocked by broken beams and piles of roof slates, and wild blackthorn crawled up the walls and bushed out into impenetrable, unkempt thickets. The few windows there were had long been robbed of their glass, and birdshit was everywhere, piled especially high in the doorway. It was as far away from a ducal manor as someone could get.

"I'm planning to kill you, and you're worried about your accommodations?" Peregrine asked, dismounting the horse. Now at the same level, Peregrine could see that Alexander's neckcloth had come loose at some point, exposing the long, lovely column of Alexander's throat. It was the kind of throat a man could spend hours licking, nuzzling.

Biting.

Peregrine had to remind his starved body that Alexander was the brother of his mortal enemy, and also the heir of the family he was determined to ruin. And also his captive.

Alexander tossed a curtain of dark hair over his shoulder

and gave Peregrine a little moue of displeasure. "I expected death. I expected torture. But I'm too beautiful and innocent for the indignity of sleeping in a building where the threshold is literally a mound of turds. Your vengeance against my family must know no bounds."

With the pout and the rumpled clothes, Alexander looked anything but innocent. He looked downright sinful. But Peregrine didn't bother to say so.

"How do you know I want revenge?" he asked instead, leading the horse—and Alexander, too, by the other end of the rope that bound him—to the low-slung stables at the side of the priory.

"I deduced it," Alexander said, sounding a little smug. Then he added, "Also, Reginald is an unholy pile of shit, so I'm not surprised someone wants to kill him. If I'm being honest, I thought this would've happened sooner."

Peregrine tied Alexander's rope to a post and then began tending to his horse, removing the bridle and replacing it with a halter to tether his mount in place. "You're not upset I plan to kill your brother?"

Alexander tilted his head, his full mouth bunched to the side. "No. I mean, I oppose the use of murder, in general, and I have no wish to be the duke, ever, ever, so I'd *rather* he not be dead. But as I've mentioned previously, he's about as wonderful as the French pox, and half as merciful."

Peregrine was used to people loathing the Duke of Jarrell around these parts, but they were all farmers, shepherds . . . *thieves.* For a lord like Alexander to admit his brother's despicable nature to someone lowborn like Peregrine was more than a breach of familial loyalty, it was a betrayal of class as well, and that was enough to make Peregrine's curiosity—and suspicion—flare.

"And," Alexander added, "you don't seem the type to do anything for any reason that's less than entirely serious, which makes me think that whatever the motive is for your revenge, I'll have some empathy for it."

Peregrine searched the finely sculpted face in front of him. The honesty he saw in those dark eyes unsettled him. Peregrine didn't want Alexander to be honest. Or empathetic.

It would . . . complicate things.

He could feel Alexander's gaze on him as he turned to hang up the saddle and then began grooming the horse, checking his mount's legs and shoes as he worked.

"I would, you know," his captive said after a minute. Softly. "Have empathy."

Peregrine didn't look up from his work.

"And if you wanted to tell me, I would listen. I would believe you."

A strange thing happened then. Peregrine's lips parted, almost as if they were ready to speak, almost as if he were ready to talk about what Reginald had done to his family after years of holding the bitter knowledge inside himself—but that couldn't be right, could it? Peregrine had been careful to never speak of his losses, even to Lyd, because if the memories cut so deeply merely in his *thoughts*, what would they do to him as words spoken aloud?

So why was he tempted to talk to this spoiled aristocrat? Why was the brother of his enemy eliciting this urge in him when his friends and fellow thieves never had?

"I don't need your belief," Peregrine said.

"Everyone needs belief."

"Not the dead," he replied, and put away the brush and pick. Then he took the horse by the halter to walk him up and down the stable aisle. He could still feel his captive's eyes burning against him as he walked.

"Are you referring to yourself?" Alexander asked. "Or to someone you lost?"

It was too close to the truth—too perceptive. Again, Peregrine felt the strange urge to speak, to explain. And along with it came a feeling that wasn't quite fear and wasn't quite resentment, but a serrated alloy of both, sharpened by the genuine honesty he heard in his prisoner's voice.

Peregrine reminded himself that Alexander was his captive right now and would likely say anything to get Peregrine to trust him, to get Peregrine to let him go.

And that, Peregrine would not do.

He didn't answer Alexander's question. And then Alexander didn't say anything else, even after Peregrine put the horse in its stall with fresh hay and water, and then unhooked his captive's rope and led him into the priory itself.

* * *

"I'M gracious enough to concede I was wrong about the ignoble lodgings."

Peregrine ignored Alexander as he led him out of the small cloister and into what used to be the priory's church. When he'd first found the priory, untouched since the Dissolution, it had been in a terrifying state. Peregrine—with the help of a few local shepherds, whom he'd paid handsomely for their future silence on the matter—had restored the back half of the building to soundness while leaving the front half alone. Which meant if someone did stumble down the narrow cart-track to the abandoned monastery, it would look even worse than unsafe—it would look worthless.

The result was a warm, dry, and bird-free space that was disguised by its ruinous frontage, an ideal hideout for Peregrine and his friends. And though they'd never bothered to take a captive before, there was plenty of room to keep one. Peregrine had the perfect place in mind: the old sacristy at the back of the church. Lyd had slept there until she started sharing one of the monk's cells with Ned, so there was already a bed and a few other amenities inside.

More importantly, there was only one high, narrow window and only one door. So long as the door was guarded, escape would be impossible.

Peregrine took Alexander there now, walking through the choir and past the uncovered altar to the sacristy. Alexander's head swiveled as they went, peering through the shadows at the piles of stolen things they hadn't had a chance to sell—bolts of cloth, bundles of leather, a basket overflowing with jewelry—and the furniture, tapestries, carpets, and candlesticks which transformed the forgotten church into a medieval hall worthy of a king.

"I'm impressed, Peregrine," the younger man said as they reached the sacristy door, and Peregrine opened it to reveal a snug, furnished room. "This is a better thieves' den than I could have imagined. Complete with piles of loot and everything. Are the stories true then? That you even have escape tunnels beneath—"

"It's not going to work," Peregrine interrupted, reaching for the lamp to light it.

Alexander gave him an innocent look. "What?"

"Manipulating me, charming me, befriending me—even trying to learn more about the priory. I know you plan to escape. And you should know that it won't work."

His captive gave him a dazzling grin. "Well, you can't blame a man for trying."

Peregrine's pulse gave an unwanted kick at the sight of Alexander's smile, and he had to look away before he did something ludicrous. Like smile back at him.

He lit the lamp and then walked over to the small fireplace.

"Get on the bed," Peregrine said gruffly.

"Oh, Peregrine, I thought you'd never ask."

Alexander's coy purr sent Peregrine's pulse jumping again, and he had to tell himself that he was a villainous highwayman who wasn't affected by the charms of a rake, no matter how lissome. No matter how pretty his throat or how long his eyelashes. Peregrine also told himself that this rake's brother had both directly and indirectly killed Peregrine's entire family.

Peregrine hated the Darthams. He hated them so much that he would happily kill all of them, even Alexander.

Right?

His mind instinctively pushed away from the idea of killing Alexander, and he decided he wasn't going to think about it right now. It wouldn't be a problem until after the ransom anyway, and so he'd think about it then. He would instead focus on the present moment, which involved somehow keeping Alexander here without his escaping.

Peregrine lit the fire, then walked over to where his captive sat perched on the edge of the bed and deftly untied his wrists. There was dirt on Alexander's knees, and his hair was in wind-blown tangles. Peregrine sighed and stepped back.

"There's a privy through that door. It opens over a rather perilous drop, so I don't recommend using it as a means of escape. I'll bring you water and fresh clothes."

Alexander blinked up at him. "That's very thoughtful. Are you this considerate of all your captives?"

"I've never had one before," Peregrine said. "I'll return briefly. Please don't make life difficult for yourself by trying to run."

"Never." Alexander swore with such earnestness that Peregrine knew he was lying. But Peregrine also remembered too vividly how it felt to go without changing clothes or washing his body when he was on a long and bitter campaign, and he wouldn't subject Alexander to that. Maybe he'd abducted him, maybe he'd kill him, but at the very least, his prisoner could be clean and comfortable.

For the time being.

Peregrine waited until Alexander went into the privy, and then he went out into the church and past the open cloister to the small, stark cell he kept for himself. He'd furnished the hideout to a high degree of comfort, but nowadays, he gave away most of the spoils to families who'd lost their livelihoods while living on Dartham lands.

After finding a clean shirt and breeches, he filled a large ewer with water from their cistern and brought it back to the sacristy. Perhaps not surprisingly, the room was empty of pouting, long-haired rakes.

With a sigh, Peregrine deposited everything on a table and then strode out of the church to the covered walkway that led to the old scriptorium and ultimately to the front of the building. The priory wasn't massive, but it had been prosperous enough to warrant several small additions over its years, which meant a labyrinthine layout. An escaping captive would have a difficult time assessing the quickest way to the front door.

Sure enough, there was a flash of red wool through the arches of the cloister, just on the other side of the garth. Peregrine hopped over the low ledge, moved through the overgrown grass in a few long bounds, and jumped into the covered walkway on the other side in time to snag Alexander by the coat.

Alexander twisted and fought, but the game was up; Peregrine had him up and over his shoulder in a moment's work. Peregrine immediately had to ignore how warm Alexander was. How firm.

How that lovely backside was currently calling for Peregrine's palm . . . or his teeth.

Alexander stopped struggling the minute Peregrine

hoisted him up, and slumped. "I thought the front door was closer," he admitted.

"It's not," Peregrine said, turning and carrying him back to the church.

"Apparently," said Alexander in a forlorn tone.

"What happened to being the best captive?"

Alexander shifted a little on Peregrine's shoulder. "I think we could debate the meaning of the word *best*, don't you? After all, from my vantage, the *best* captive would be the captive who doesn't miss an opportunity to run."

Peregrine's voice was wry when he spoke. "And from my vantage?"

Alexander paused. "Well, obviously the best captive for you would be someone lively and interesting. Entertaining. To relieve you of boredom, of course."

"Of course."

Peregrine walked through the doorway and then dropped Alexander on the bed, where the young man lay with his limbs spread like a starfish, blinking up at the ceiling.

"Is this what my captivity is going to be?" Alexander asked. "You hauling me around like a sack of grain?"

Peregrine didn't answer and instead gestured to the clothes and ewer. "I will be standing outside the door. I recommend you wash and change as I do. You'll be more comfortable."

Alexander hoisted himself up on an elbow, eyebrow curved in provocative suggestion. "More comfortable for what? Because I have some ideas."

Alexander was too playful like this, too *bright*. Just looking at him on the bed, with his eyes glittering and his mouth quirked, made Peregrine's blood feel like it was made of fire. It made Peregrine feel, period.

That was a problem, since Peregrine preferred only one feeling, and that was hatred of the Darthams. That hatred had been his only purpose, his single cold solace these last four years, and it was going to stay that way, no matter how playful or pretty this Dartham heir was.

With a shake of his head, Peregrine left the room, leaving the heavy shape of his own silence behind him.

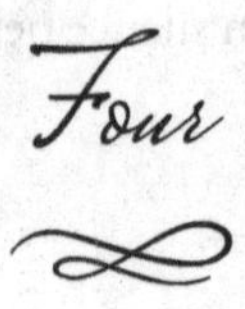

Four

SANDY

SANDY RATHER WISHED he'd been able to escape, but he had to admit to himself that the last three hours of his life had been livelier and more interesting than the last three years put together, which probably also meant that he should admit to himself that the last few years of his life had been rather unsatisfying. Decadent, certainly, but in a way that increased his restlessness rather than soothing it.

Maybe he'd needed a good adventure to shake things up a little.

And while there was the small, pesky matter of Peregrine planning to kill him, Sandy still felt certain he could either escape or seduce his way free. Which . . . given the way it felt to be slung over the brawny highwayman's shoulder earlier, Sandy wouldn't mind in the least having to do some seduction. He'd seen Peregrine's body fighting its response to his own the whole ride here, and he'd caught Peregrine staring at his mouth once or twice—or thirty times. The idea of unraveling that cold, grim mystery . . . well.

It wasn't without its own appeal.

After all, if he lived to tell the tale, what was a bigger coup for a rake than being in a highwayman's bed? Even the hedonistic denizens of the Second Kingdom couldn't boast something that wild.

Sandy washed with a linen towel and some very chilly water and then changed into the clothes the highwayman had brought him. They were clean, but soft with wear and too big for his frame, which was shorter and more slender than Peregrine Hind's. The breeches settled low around his hips, and the shirt opened nearly to his sternum.

He should have felt ridiculous like this, but he didn't at all. He felt rather snug, actually—cared for. Which was an absurd thought to have about wearing a captor's clothes. But they even smelled like the highwayman, like rain and like leather. Sandy found himself breathing deep to take the scent into his lungs, and then he wanted to shake himself. Very hard.

Because it was one thing for seduction not to be a chore, but it was another thing entirely to swoon over his jailer, *even if* that jailer was unfairly worthy of swoons. Even if that jailer had eyes like moonlight itself.

Which was funny. Sandy couldn't remember ever caring about a lover's eyes before.

Not a lover! he reminded himself. *Captor*. Future *murderer*. It wouldn't do to forget that part!

Sandy was combing his hair when Peregrine knocked—a silly but almost endearing gesture, given the circumstances— and Sandy called for him to enter. Peregrine stepped in and then stilled.

"You may finish," the highwayman said, his voice devoid of inflection. But Sandy saw the swallow of the thief's throat as he watched Sandy pull the comb through his dark locks. "I don't mind."

"So generous," Sandy murmured, finishing up and then

tossing his hair over his shoulder as he regarded the impassive man standing before him. "However, I have to ask about what you plan on doing with me next. Am I to be kept in this room combing my hair forever? Like a mortal woman trapped in a fairy castle?"

"Not quite," Peregrine said. "On the bed. Again."

Sandy was about to make another sly remark when he saw what Peregrine had been hiding behind his back. Not coils of rough rope like he'd used to tie Sandy's wrists earlier, but several lengths of what appeared to be silk.

Delicious images sloshed around Sandy's mind like wine in a glass. "Oh," he said.

"On the bed, Alexander."

Sandy felt strange as he obeyed—full of dread and excitement and a heady mixture of both—and then he realized, as Peregrine stepped to the edge of the bed and took hold of his wrist, that he was trembling.

Peregrine met his gaze. "I won't leave you tied up forever," he said, misunderstanding the reason for Sandy's shivers. "The others are returning, and I need to speak with them, which means we won't have a guard at the door. And obviously you can't be trusted, even for an hour or two."

"Obviously," Sandy said weakly, his heart thumping against his ribs as Peregrine cinched the silk around his wrist and then around the nearest poster of the bed. Then Peregrine moved to the other wrist, and then to a bare ankle, tying his knots firmly but not so tightly that Sandy lost feeling in his fingers or toes.

Sandy knew there was no hiding his fast-heaving chest, his hot cheeks, and above all, the insistent erection pushing against the front of his borrowed breeches, but it wasn't until the highwayman was tying Sandy's last ankle to the bed that he looked up from his work and saw what it had done to his captive.

Peregrine's lips parted, and then his silver eyes shot to Sandy's face—in confusion or in accusation, Sandy couldn't tell.

"I told you I liked being tied up," Sandy said as he twisted against his bonds, testing them. Every twist pulled at the fabric of the too-loose shirt, and so, as Peregrine watched, Sandy's stomach above the waistband of the breeches was exposed inch by quivering inch. Along with the swollen head of his cock, which peeked rudely above the waistband and leaked onto Sandy's belly.

"You like being tied up," Peregrine repeated tonelessly.

Sandy wanted so dearly to make a face at him but was too aroused to pull it off. The tightness of the restraints, the spread position of his limbs, the sheer *helplessness*—it created a tide so deep and so urgent inside him that it was pointless to resist. It would be like fighting off the pleasure in a dream, or a release inside a lover's mouth.

He would lose—and it was more fun to lose, anyway.

Peregrine's face expressed nothing as he tied the final knot, but as he straightened, Sandy could see a new tightness to the way he moved. His face remained unreadable, but his hands were curling into slow fists, and his eyes had gone more black than silver.

He looked like—well, for an instant, he looked like he wanted to eat Sandy alive.

He left without another word.

* * *

SANDY DIDN'T MAKE it long. With his bindings, the intoxicating smell of the highwayman wrapping around him, and the waistband of the breeches rubbing lightly against the underside of his prick, it was a foregone conclusion that he would spend all over his stomach, and he did. Sandy spent with long, jerking spills as he thought of the highwayman's pale eyes and big hands.

He stared up at the ceiling in a daze, wondering how long Peregrine would leave him like this and how long he could stand it. *Not forever* wasn't a very precise amount of time, and from what he could hear through the door, the other thieves had only just now made it to the sanctuary. He heard the clanking of cups and smelled the aroma of hot food, and then heard the low din of conversation.

What are they talking about? What to do with him while they waited to be paid his ransom? How to kill him once they had?

He wouldn't be there to be killed, of course, having weaseled or fucked his way free, but he did wonder how Peregrine felt about killing him.

Would he feel reluctant, maybe? Remorseful but resigned?

It was a shame they'd met like this because Sandy would've very much enjoyed being tied to a bed by Peregrine Hind on a regular basis. But after Sandy escaped, it would probably be best if he never ran into Peregrine or his eerie eyes again, for the obvious not-being-murdered-for-revenge reasons.

A tragic thought.

Sandy tried to make himself focus on possible avenues of escape while he waited for the thieves to finish talking. He'd peered through the privy hole earlier, and it had indeed led to a steep drop, and the sacristy window was too narrow to be of any use. His only way out was through the door, which was possibly guarded, and he already knew he'd be no good at fighting off a guard.

No, he'd need to stick to his strengths. Seduction, lying . . . bravado and charm.

The woman thief might be the ripest possibility. If only he could remember where he knew her from. Was she a former lover? A friend of a lover? Someone connected to the Second Kingdom?

But Sandy's mind didn't stay on escape for very long. It was impossible to think clearly while tied up like this, smelling rain and leather and knowing Peregrine would walk in eventually and see that Sandy had spilled all over himself. What would Peregrine do when he did? Would he fix Sandy with that look, that hot, hungry look? Would he get hard? Would he reach out and touch Sandy with one of those big, rough hands . . . ?

Lost in his imaginings, Sandy didn't notice the door opening until it was shutting again and Peregrine was inside. Peregrine's legs were long enough and the room was small enough that it only took him three good strides to make it to the side of the bed, and even in his lust-induced haze, Sandy noticed how quick and silent those strides were. Peregrine could move like a ghost when he wanted.

The highwayman seemed to take in Sandy's half-lidded eyes, his quivering limbs, the spatter of semen on his belly. His eyes dropped to Sandy's renewed erection, which surged happily at the attention.

"You've already spent," Peregrine said after a moment. "And you're still like this?"

"I *told* you," Sandy said, meaning to sound indignant but sounding breathless instead. "I *like* being tied up."

Peregrine's hand stretched out, and then they both watched as he dropped his fingertips to the top of Sandy's knee, right above the hem of the breeches. His fingertips rested there, over the woolen broadcloth, pressing lightly against the place where the muscles of Sandy's thigh anchored to his femur. And then, agonizingly, Peregrine trailed his fingers up, up, up to Sandy's hip.

Peregrine looked as if even he didn't know what he was doing, like he was encountering a treasure he had no idea how to steal, and Sandy was too drunk with desire to tell him this wasn't stealing. This wasn't even seduction, if he was being honest.

It was desperation.

"Please," Sandy whispered. "*Please*."

Peregrine gave him a sharp look, and Sandy realized that he must sound like he had earlier, in the middle of the road, when he was pleading for his life.

But this was something much, much more important.

Sandy lifted his hips as much as the restraints would allow, trying to twist into Peregrine's hand, which stayed resolutely unmoving against Sandy's hip. "Please."

Peregrine's mouth was a straight line. But his eyes—he couldn't hide those hungry, blown-pupil eyes. He couldn't hide the way he swallowed over and over, as if searching for control.

"Why should I?" the highwayman finally asked.

Good question. Why should he pleasure a captive—a captive he planned on killing, and who was the brother of someone he clearly hated? Sandy blurted the first thing he could think of.

"Revenge?"

Peregrine's fingers lifted and then ghosted lightly over the inseam of the breeches, running over the place where Sandy's testicles had drawn up tight to his body. "How is this revenge for *me*?"

"Umm," Sandy said, and then added an "*Ohhhhh*" when Peregrine's fingers moved up to wander around the base of his cock. Sandy's erection bobbed, the crown dripping clear seed and burning like hot iron in the cool air.

"Well, it's humiliating," Sandy mumbled. "I'm so humiliated right now. Please, Peregrine. Please."

Peregrine's eyes flashed with some indecipherable emotion, but whatever it was had him bracing one knee on the bed as he tore at the buttons holding the breeches closed. In an instant, Sandy's prick was completely naked and then there was the hand of his abductor wrapping tight around him and stroking hard.

Sandy's back nearly bowed off the bed, even with his limbs tied, and never had he felt so helpless, so depraved, as when the man who was going to kill him was pumping his prick with a hard and vicious fist. When the release came, it felt like it was pulled right from his spine, right from the very marrow of his bones. He spurted seed all over the highwayman's fingers, all over his stomach again, and the highwayman didn't seem to mind at all, seemed to like it, in fact, because by the time Sandy's body was drained totally dry, Peregrine's cheeks were flushed and his shaft was very visibly thickened in his breeches.

His eyes met Sandy's, and Sandy saw shock there, and lust, and several other things besides. Peregrine staggered back from the bed, his hand still covered in the milky proof of Sandy's release, and he stared at that hand as if he wasn't sure how he'd ended up like this.

"I can return the favor," Sandy murmured. "You don't even have to untie me. You could use my mouth."

Peregrine shuddered, the flush deepening on his cheeks, and Sandy knew he'd found a weakness. Peregrine wanted inside his mouth. Badly.

Maybe even other places . . .

But a huge crash resounded from outside the sacristy door, followed by roars of laughter, and Peregrine seemed to snap out of whatever spell had overtaken him. With a sharp shake of his head, the highwayman walked over to the table and, using the ewer and a fresh towel, cleaned his hand. Then he came over to Sandy and wiped Sandy's messy stomach clean.

The thickness in the thief's breeches was unabated, but Peregrine didn't unbutton them to relieve his desire, and he didn't—as Sandy secretly hoped—climb onto the bed next to

Sandy and make use of him. Instead, the thief began untying him, loosening the knots and then checking to make sure Sandy could still move his fingers and toes.

When he was completely untied, Sandy sat up and stared at him. "Let me make you feel better with my mouth," he said. "I'm very good at it."

Peregrine bundled the lengths of silk into neat coils as the silence after Sandy's offer filled the room. The highwayman's eyes glittered behind his lowered lashes—glittered with something less than vengeance and something more than lust. Secret things that made Sandy's pulse speed up. Finally Peregrine said brusquely, "I'm your captor."

"I thought we went over this," Sandy said impatiently. "It's revenge. You're getting revenge and stuff."

"Maybe. Or maybe you're trying to seduce your way free."

"Well, that sounds like a winning scenario for both of us!"

Peregrine leveled a look at him.

Sandy did his best to look innocent, but the effect was doubtful since he'd just done very *not* innocent things all over his stomach. "Did I mention that I'm so very good at it and also how vengeful you'll feel while it's happening?"

"Good night, Alexander," the highwayman said. "There will be a guard outside your door tonight. I'll make sure they bring in some food and wine for you too."

A sharp displeasure sliced through Sandy at the thought of Peregrine leaving. He wanted more bed-play, yes, but he also just wanted his captor *here*, with him. He wasn't sure why, exactly. Maybe it had something to do with those secrets shimmering in the highwayman's silver eyes.

"Peregrine!" Sandy called, but there was no reply. His captor had gone.

Five

PEREGRINE

FOR AS LONG AS he lived, Peregrine would never forget the way Alexander looked while tied to a bed, hair tousled and gleaming in the lamplight, his stomach pearled with his orgasm. And for as long as he lived, he'd never forget the way Alexander's cock felt as he stroked it. Hotter than a brand, harder than steel. Yet soft and velvety too, like pure heaven in his hand.

For the sake of his own sanity, Peregrine didn't take a shift guarding Alexander's door that night or the next morning. He didn't think he could listen to Alexander rustling around in bed or sighing his put-upon sighs, and he didn't know how he'd respond if Alexander came to the door and tried to talk to him.

No. He *did* know how he'd respond. He'd push his way through that door and shove Alexander back onto the bed. And this time he wouldn't leave Alexander's cell with a cock-stand still straining his pants.

Let me make you feel better.

I'm so very good at it.

Instead, Peregrine went to his cell and slept a little, waking with the sun to begin working his way through a list of things needing to be fenced soon. He'd been marking the papers for less than an hour when he heard a knock at the door.

"Yes?" he called.

Will, the youngest of their band and the person guarding Alexander today, pushed his head into the room. "Lord Alexander says he can't fall back asleep because his bed linens are too scratchy."

Peregrine stared. "Too scratchy?"

Will shrugged.

"I suppose," Peregrine said slowly, "he could have some other bed linens if we have them."

"Thanks," Will said, and then left the room and closed the door behind him. Peregrine shook his head and then went back to the inventory sheets, unsure if captives were supposed to complain about their bed linens, but also certain that it probably didn't matter, since Alexander had already proved himself to be a deeply vexing captive.

Let me make you feel better.

Well, perhaps not entirely vexing.

A few hours later, Peregrine was eating lunch in his room and finishing his tallies when he heard another knock. It was Will again.

"Yes?" Peregrine asked as the thief stepped into his room.

"Alexander says he doesn't like the beer we've served with his lunch and wants wine instead. Is that permissible?"

"Yes," Peregrine said, his patience fraying a little. "That's *permissible.*"

Not ten minutes later, Will was back. "Alexander says his wine is too sweet and he wants to know if we have a more mature vintage."

Peregrine tossed his quill on the table in exasperation.

"No. You may tell Lord Alexander that he'll be drinking water from the trough if he has any more complaints about his beverages."

Will looked at little surprised at Peregrine's flare of temper—and Peregrine was surprised too. He never let his emotions creep toward the surface, even with his closest friends. Lyd, who still only knew the scantest details of why he wanted to kill Reginald Dartham, who had never seen him seethe in anger or weep in the dark—or even laugh.

It was safer that way, and better for all involved.

But with Alexander Dartham, Peregrine's curated restraint unglued itself. His lapse in control last night, his irritation today . . .

The spoiled rake was taking Peregrine apart bit by bit. If only he'd stop being so *here*, so *present*, so impossible to ignore—but there was no ignoring Lord Alexander Dartham. There were those dark eyes and that full mouth, there was his unabashed vulnerability, the way he asked for things and tried for things.

There was his earnestness, equally unabashed, as if it had never occurred to him to lie, even about something as gravely important as escaping.

With a cautious nod, Will left to give Alexander his answer, and Peregrine scrubbed his hands over his face. He had to find more control when it came to Alexander Dartham. Otherwise, he'd be entirely undone by the time he received the ransom from the duke, and he didn't know how he'd be able to do what he needed to do after—

No. He wouldn't think about that right now.

A hundred things could happen between now and then, and he needed to keep his focus on the duke instead.

Speaking of, he stood and left his cell in search of Lyd to see if there'd been any messages from Chagford. He found her in the sanctuary, her head bent over a note.

"News from Far Hope?" he asked, suddenly anxious about the answer. If it was news from Far Hope, if the duke was going to pay the ransom, then that meant Peregrine would have no more use for Alexander. It meant Alexander would become a liability rather than an asset and his death would become Peregrine's best weapon for hurting the duke—

His mind reared away from those thoughts like a shying horse, and he drew in a relieved breath when Lyd said, "Nothing from the duke yet. But our friend in Exeter sent this." She waved the note, an avid glitter to her blue eyes. "The duchess is leaving for Far Hope. She hadn't felt well enough to travel yesterday and that's why she didn't go with her husband or Sandy."

"You want to intercept her," Peregrine guessed.

"Yes," Lyd said.

"To rob her?" Peregrine asked. There was no judgment in his tone, only curiosity. He was keeping a captive, after all, and planning that captive's murder, so he hardly had a moral high ground here.

Nor did he want one.

Lyd's jaw tightened. "I don't know," she admitted after a moment. "After everything she's done to me, robbing doesn't feel like enough."

When he'd first met Lydia, she'd been pickpocketing in London, one in a thousand thieves struggling to survive. But when she'd made the mistake of pickpocketing *him*, she'd done it so adroitly and with so much fearlessness that Peregrine had been more impressed than annoyed. He'd offered her a job as a fellow knight of the road, and she'd accepted, with the caveat that any Dartham they came across would be hers.

He'd been astounded that someone else could hate that family as much as he, but after hearing Lyd's story, he'd recognized a kindred spirit. A distant cousin of the duchess, she'd been shipped off to live with the duke and duchess after her parents had died of smallpox, and they'd attempted to marry her off at sixteen to a cruel man. When she'd refused, the duchess had locked Lyd in her room for weeks, keeping her a prisoner until Lyd managed to escape through a window. Lyd maintained that scraping out an existence as a thief—even as a woman alone, and in the rough crowds of London—had been infinitely preferable to marrying the person the duchess had chosen for her.

The duchess had been adamant about the match because the suitor in question would take Lyd without a dowry, which meant the dowry and the family property Lyd was supposed to bring to a future marriage would stay in the hands of the duke and duchess. That property included Lyd's family home and her family land—the very place she'd grown up. A place she would never see again while it belonged to the Darthams.

"What she's taken from you is something impossible to replace," Peregrine said to Lyd now. "I understand why robbing her of some clothes or jewelry wouldn't feel like enough."

Lyd swore, looking out over their piles of fabric and silver goods. "Sometimes I want so much to hurt her," she said after a minute. "But other times I don't know what I'd do if I saw her again. If I'd have it in me to hurt her after all."

"I understand," Peregrine said. Lord Alexander Dartham was the still-living proof of that. "Do you know if she's leaving today or tomorrow?"

Lyd shook her head.

"You may want to plan on watching the road for a day or two, then. Pack food and take Ned and the others. I'll stay here with our prisoner."

She looked at him. "You'd rather stay with the brother of your enemy than go out to *rob* your enemy's wife? Are you sure you're still Peregrine Hind, infamous highwayman?"

Will trotted up before Peregrine could answer, looking a

little sheepish for interrupting. "Sandy wants to know if you have any books here."

"*Sandy?*" Peregrine repeated. "He's Sandy to you now?"

"*Books?*" Lyd asked at the same time.

Will held up his hands, as if indicating helplessness in the face of the circumstances. "He says he needs to occupy his mind, and we did play All Fours for a bit, but he kept winning and said it wasn't challenging enough to be any fun."

"Are you sure he was winning and not cheating?" Lyd asked, the doubt clear in her voice.

Peregrine sighed, his irritation flaring all over again. "I'll assume care of our prisoner for now. Lyd, take the others. And ride safe."

* * *

A FEW MINUTES LATER, Peregrine knocked on the door of Alexander's sacristy.

"Enter," came the magnanimous reply, and Peregrine pushed open the door to see his prisoner on the bed, lounging on one elbow. The borrowed shirt exposed a sculpted shoulder and the curve of his collarbone, both illuminated by the window high on the wall. His hair was still sleep-tousled, and his feet were bare; his shirt was rucked up enough that Peregrine could see the dark line of hair leading down from his navel.

He looked like someone had spent the night fucking him into the mattress.

"You want books," Peregrine said.

"I'm bored," whined Alexander.

You're trouble. But Peregrine didn't say it. Instead, he said, "The others are leaving, but I'm staying here. I think you'll find that I'm less amenable to requests for things."

Alexander dropped his head back with a fractious noise. "But it's so *dull* in here. What else am I to do?"

"You're a captive," Peregrine said impatiently. "Your entire existence is to wait until something happens."

Alexander sat up. "Play cards with me."

"No."

"Why not?"

"You'll cheat."

"If I did," Alexander said, giving him a mischievous grin, "you could always punish me."

A slow bloom of heat unfurled inside Peregrine. His voice was graveled with it when he spoke. "And how would I do that?"

"You could tie me up again," Alexander said, coming to a sitting position and then to his knees. He kept his eyes on Peregrine's the entire time. "You could tie me up all sorts of ways, you know, not just on my back. On my stomach, or bent over the bed, or . . ."

Peregrine had to swallow to keep himself from agreeing. Or tackling Alexander to the bed and finally putting his lips to the full curves of Alexander's mouth.

It would be so much easier if Alexander weren't so playful, so goddamn *happy*. When was the last time Peregrine himself had felt playful?

Happy?

"I will be tying you up again," he said, deciding then and there what he'd do with his captive today. He told himself it was for practical, preventing-escape reasons, and not at all for reasons of seeing Alexander bound in silk. "But not to the bed. Come with me."

* * *

FOUR HOURS LATER, they were alone in the sanctuary as the light slowly died outside and the shadows began to gather in the corners. Peregrine had bound Alexander's hands and then had dragged him along while he attended to the day's tasks—caring for the horses and fixing the wheel on one of the carts they used to haul goods to Chagford or Buckfast, and then finally making a simple dinner of roasted pheasant, apples, and bread for them to eat.

The playfulness hadn't left Peregrine's captive as Peregrine had worked, and Lord Alexander had spent most of the afternoon perched on a barrel, kicking his bare feet against the wood while he pestered Peregrine with an unceasing number of questions about everything from hay to types of hammers to when Peregrine would take pity on him and at least let Alexander bring himself to satisfaction.

Each time Alexander asked that last question, Peregrine couldn't keep himself from looking over at his captive—all sparkling eyes and breeches obscenely tented from the effects of having his wrists bound—and it would nearly stop his heart. It was like having a spoiled princeling about, and Peregrine should hate it, should hate the pretty pouts and the coy demands, but the honesty shining in those impish glances and scrawled inside those flirtatious questions made hate impossible.

In fact, Peregrine felt lighter and lighter as the afternoon went on, like Alexander was a glow of lamplight in a room he hadn't realized had grown dim. And seeing Alexander aroused from being tied up, with those half-lidded eyes and flush-stained cheeks . . .

Repeatedly, Peregrine had to remind himself that Alexander was a *Dartham*, and moreover, his captive. He shouldn't feel anything but grimly determined while he was around. He shouldn't have to catch his breath whenever he saw his captive lord staring at his silk-trussed wrists with fascination and undisguised arousal.

When it was time for dinner, Peregrine tied the free end of Alexander's rope to the arm of his chair and then watched as, despite his bindings and his visible erection, his captive ate as prettily as if he were in front of the Queen herself. In contrast, Peregrine himself ate quickly and efficiently, an inevitable consequence of war and four years on the run from the law.

"You eat like a soldier," said Alexander after a moment.

"I was a soldier," Peregrine said somewhat automatically, and then immediately wanted to unspeak the words. He knew Alexander was trying to learn anything useful that would help him escape while also ingratiating himself through any means possible, including friendship. Peregrine probably shouldn't even be eating with him now, if he was honest, but it was nicer than eating alone, and Alexander was so very lovely to look at, and sometimes he said the funniest things.

Sometimes he almost made Peregrine smile.

"Of course you were," Alexander said. "And now you're a knight of the road. Isn't that how all the stories start? A valiant soldier returns home after the war and finds his home taken away from him, and so the only recourse he has is to steal from the very men who robbed him in the first place?"

It was too close to the truth, and Peregrine struggled not to react. "You're thinking of Robin Hood, or maybe the Royalists after the Civil War," he said carefully. "Times long past."

Alexander didn't seem to miss how Peregrine sidestepped his remark, however. "So what then makes a modern-day soldier take to the road?"

"What makes the son of a duke spend his days carousing and cheating at cards?"

"I never cheat, I only *strategize*," Alexander said, taking a dainty sip of wine. "And it's more nights than days, you know."

"But there's no other work your brother would rather put you to? No responsibilities waiting for you at Far Hope?"

Alexander's expression shuttered, and it was as if a light had gone out. He didn't like this line of questioning any more than Peregrine had liked Alexander's.

"There's plenty waiting for me at Far Hope," Alexander said cryptically.

He set down his cup and turned to face Peregrine. On the far side of the room, the fire burned in its improvised fireplace and cast Alexander's elegant features in a reddish glow.

"What?" Peregrine asked his captive, who was now staring at him with an unsettling expression.

"I was just thinking," Alexander said in a velvet voice, "that I should show you why it's worthwhile to keep a rake nearby."

A dark heat crawled up Peregrine's thighs and down his belly. He should ignore it; he knew he should. But it burned so very hot inside him. It had been kindled and stoked by seeing Alexander so coquettish all day, and Peregrine couldn't remember the last time he'd felt like this. Maybe he never had.

"Is that so?" Peregrine asked in a gruff voice.

Alexander gave him a secretive smile. He slid easily from his bench to his knees, graceful as a dancer. Within a few sinuous crawls, he was in front of Peregrine's chair.

Peregrine knew he should tell Alexander to stop, to go back to his bench. But he didn't. He couldn't.

Instead, he angled his chair and spread his legs, feeling his control slip and slip and slip as his captive moved between his feet.

Alexander brought his bound hands up between them. Peregrine had tied them so that they were separated by a few inches of silk—so he could still eat and use the privy without help—but now his captive held them folded together, like he was praying. Like he was supplicating Peregrine for a favor.

"Let me taste you," Alexander said, his voice a low, wonderful purr that no doubt had wooed many men and women to his bed over the years. "How long has it been since you've had your cock sucked, Peregrine?"

Too long, Peregrine thought, but he didn't answer out loud. He did another thing that he absolutely should not have and untucked Alexander's shirt, so he could lift it and see underneath. So he could see if Alexander's organ was pushing against his breeches like it had been last night.

It was.

"If you're wondering if I am inflamed," Alexander said, somewhat dryly, "the answer is yes."

"Is it because your hands are bound, or because you sincerely wish to do this?"

Alexander peered up at him through dark lashes. "Why can't it be both? If it comforts you, I'd want to do it even if I wasn't your captive," he added. "Please, Peregrine. Just a little. Just a taste. Let me taste you."

Peregrine didn't know how to say no to this. He needed to say no—Alexander's family had *killed* the only people he'd ever loved—and aside from that very large consideration, he wasn't the kind of man to use someone else for pleasure when that someone else was a prisoner.

But Alexander's hands were so warm through the fabric of his shirt as they pressed against his stomach, as they slowly plucked at the linen until it was completely untucked and the buttons of his breeches were exposed. And Alexander's eyes were so pretty like this, glittering under their dark fringe of lashes, and his mouth looked so soft, and knowing that he was hard as he knelt between Peregrine's feet . . .

And then Peregrine's breeches were unbuttoned and his cock was free, heavy and tumescent and pointing at the ceiling.

Alexander's exhales shivered over the sensitive skin of Peregrine's shaft, sending bolts of sensation right through his body and making him swell even more. The skin stretched over his crown was so tight that it shone in the firelight.

His captive gave him a wicked grin. "I think you might need this."

Peregrine grunted. He did, but this was the last person whom he should take it from, and—*oh God*. Alexander's tongue ran a wet stripe up his cock and Peregrine nearly fainted. With another wicked grin, Alexander bent over him and took him into his hot, slick mouth.

Peregrine had forgotten. Fuck, he'd forgotten. How it felt to be inside a lover's mouth, and how much better it was than his own perfunctory hand. He'd forgotten everything else that came with a moment like this—Alexander's gorgeous hair spilling over Peregrine's lap, and the soft noises he made as he sucked, and the flirtatious flicks of his gaze up at Peregrine, as if to say, *See? See? Aren't I so good at this?*

He couldn't be sure if it was his hatred of the Darthams or concern for Alexander that made him press his fingers under Alexander's chin and force Alexander to pull away from his work, but whatever it was, it twisted inside Peregrine like smoke off a bonfire, billowing and thick. "This doesn't change anything," he told the younger man. "This *won't* change anything."

"It won't?" Alexander asked innocently. His lips were wet and slightly swollen from pleasuring Peregrine, and Peregrine couldn't take it anymore.

He leaned forward to kiss his kidnapped rake.

Alexander's mouth tasted of wine and sex, and it was so sweet on Peregrine's tongue, so silky and inviting. Alexander's tongue fluttered gently against Peregrine's, almost like he was surprised, and then he whimpered as Peregrine deepened the kiss, plundering Alexander's mouth like it was a chest of valuables stashed under a carriage seat. He stroked his tongue against Alexander's and then bit gently at his lower lip before pulling back.

"I'm not going to set you free, no matter how good you suck me."

"Hmm," Alexander said, a sly curve to his mouth. "Maybe not. Maybe you'll decide to keep me instead."

Before Peregrine could figure out how he felt about that idea, Alexander's hair was spilling all over Peregrine's lap once more, and his tongue was doing something incredible around his slit, and then Peregrine was inside Alexander's mouth again, feeling pressure and suction and wet, wet heat.

The peak that gathered inside Peregrine's belly was ferocious and frightening—the kind of peak that would tear through him like a musket ball if he let it. And he was going to let it, because Alexander had been right: he was very, *very* good at this.

Just as his thighs tensed, Alexander looked up and met Peregrine's eyes. In the dim room, the dark sapphire of the rake's gaze was nearly impossible to make out, but Peregrine still had the strange feeling that he was seeing the color of something very important.

Something like the color of happiness itself.

His cock swelled against Alexander's tongue and began pulsing seed deep into his throat—which Alexander seemed to relish swallowing, because he didn't stop until Peregrine's cock was completely sated, and Peregrine was drained of every last drop.

Peregrine's head dropped back, his heart beating fast, his body trembling. Never, not even in a soldier's tent on the Continent, had he been so expertly and enthusiastically pleasured.

Alexander knew it too, because when Peregrine finally

looked back down at his captive, there was a smug expression on his lovely face.

"Told you," Alexander said.

"You did tell me," Peregrine agreed, turning to the knot that held Alexander's bindings to his chair. Alexander watched him with the smugness fading into confusion, and then he laughed as Peregrine stood up and swung him over his shoulder.

"I didn't even have to escape this time to get carried off by my big, bad highwayman," he teased as Peregrine grabbed a candlestick with his free hand and then strode into the sacristy.

He dropped Alexander unceremoniously onto the bed, then set the candlestick down. "Clothes off," Peregrine said. "If you'd like."

"Oh, I'd always *like*," Alexander purred. "I only have one request."

Peregrine slanted him a look. "Softer sheets? Better wine? *Books?*"

"No," Alexander said with another grin the devil himself wouldn't have been able to match for its mischief. "I want your clothes off too."

Six

SANDY

TO SANDY'S GREAT DISAPPOINTMENT,
Peregrine didn't fulfill his most delicious wish of being fucked
while still trussed up, but he did crawl over Sandy with those
broad shoulders and those muscle-swollen thighs and push
Sandy's bound hands above his head. And then he'd
proceeded to kiss Sandy so thoroughly that Sandy was certain
he was now ruined for all other kisses for the rest of his life.

Sandy knew what his best friend Juliana would say—that
he'd made similar claims in the past, and they'd all fallen
equally flat. Sandy had a great weakness for other rakes and
rakesses, and often found himself the seduc-*ee* rather than the
seduc-*er*. He usually knew when he was being seduced for
someone else's amusement—being a rake himself made him
quite clear-eyed when it came to such things—but he
frequently surrendered himself to the melodrama of a love
affair anyway, simply because it was fun and because he was
bored.

But this was different somehow.

This wasn't a seduction, and there was nothing jaded or amused about the way Peregrine Hind kissed him. There was a solidity to Peregrine's touches, a gravity, and Sandy craved the weight of them. He loved the way those touches pulled on his heart and on his breath.

Sandy came with Peregrine's mouth hot and sucking on his neck and their erections trapped between their stomachs. Peregrine followed him soon after.

After Peregrine had untied him and cleaned them both, he laid back down on the bed next to Sandy. Sandy's heart stuttered as the highwayman ran his fingertips over Sandy's mouth, his pale eyes burning into Sandy's. What was Peregrine thinking right now? What was he feeling and wanting? More touching? More sex?

Did he want to tell Sandy—again—that this didn't change anything?

The idea of that was unbearable. "The best part of being in bed with a rake is that I don't expect you to croon sweet nothings to me after," Sandy informed Peregrine.

The highwayman just gave him a bland look.

"Do I seem like the type to croon sweet nothings?" Peregrine asked after a pause.

"Well. No," Sandy admitted. Peregrine seemed like the type to be found taming a wild horse up in the hills, or perhaps completing some quest that involved trudging through a barren wasteland and killing a dragon or something. There was nothing sweet about him. He was all flint and chill, with only rare glimpses of the deeply banked fire within.

But Sandy liked that about Peregrine Hind—perhaps more than was good for him—and instead of pleasuring Peregrine into a sleep deep enough for an escape attempt, Sandy propped himself up on an elbow so he could watch Peregrine's face. "Then why are you in here still?"

A pause. "I don't know."

"You don't know?"

The highwayman frowned. "I suppose I don't want to leave."

"A common reaction to my company," Sandy replied with a grin. He slid his hand down to Peregrine's cock to play it with it, thinking that was the real reason Peregrine hadn't wanted to leave, but Peregrine caught his wrist and stopped him.

Sandy froze. That was a first, and it couldn't be because Peregrine *wasn't* interested in more bed-play—his cock was already stirring for more. But Peregrine seemed to ignore it, his eyes on Sandy's face.

"Why didn't you want to talk about Far Hope?" he asked. "Before, when I'd asked about it?"

Far Hope.

The question was so surprising that Sandy couldn't even think of a way to deflect. He looked up into a veiled expression belied by an avid, searching gaze. That gaze betrayed something haunted and yet miserably alive, locked deep under the surface like living fire beneath the earth. But there was more than pain in the highwayman's eyes. There was something that spoke of surviving, of prevailing.

Of strength, maybe.

Suddenly Sandy found that he didn't *want* to deflect.

"Your voice is pure Devonshire," Sandy said after a minute. "Did you grow up near Far Hope?"

Peregrine's expression remained unreadable. "Close enough."

"I don't suppose you've heard any of the rumors about it? About what happens there?"

"My mother once said that they keep their own ways at Far Hope," Peregrine said. "I'd always assumed it meant the Dartham selfishness was congenital."

Sandy wanted to be wounded by that, but the truth was

that his father had been a selfish and cruel man, and Reginald had inherited every drop of that selfishness and cruelty right along with the title.

At least Sandy wasn't willfully cruel. Or so he hoped.

"It means there are secrets at Far Hope," Sandy said, "and they all branch out from this one: there is a hidden kingdom inside the one we live in. It has many of the same citizens, but it's invisible and it's never spoken of to outsiders."

Peregrine regarded him. "Then why are you speaking of it to me?"

"Because I want to, and because—this feels ridiculous to say, given that you're planning to kill me—I trust you. Besides, I can always claim you tortured it out of me, if I survive this."

"If you survive this," Peregrine echoed, his voice betraying nothing, no confirmation . . . or refutation either.

Sandy planned on escaping before the matter of his survival became a pressing issue, but a small arrow of hurt—a lover's hurt—burrowed between his ribs at the realization that Peregrine still intended to kill him. Silly, since his eventual death had been the bargain struck from the very beginning. But Sandy had grown so fascinated by this bleak force of a man, become so strangely affectionate toward him, and he childishly wanted Peregrine to feel the same way. Less for reasons of survival than for reasons that were perilously rooted in the organ beating in his chest.

"Anyway," Sandy said, pushing all that away and down, down where he wouldn't have to feel it right then, "this hidden kingdom is centuries old. Maybe older. And though its citizens are all over the island, Far Hope is its seat, its ancestral home."

"What's the purpose of this kingdom?" Peregrine asked.

Sandy scoffed. "What's the purpose of any kingdom? To continue to exist, of course."

Peregrine tucked his arm behind his head, the better to

look at Sandy, and the gesture was so casual, so familiar and *cozy*, that Sandy's chest gave an unexpected squeeze.

"I know what you're really asking, though," Sandy continued, "and the Second Kingdom has no political ambitions, no designs for more wealth or power—or at least, it's not supposed to. It's supposed to be a place where people associate freely for pleasure alone. That is our raison d'être, in fact. No law but pleasure. No limit but acquiescence. No rule but secrecy."

"This sounds like a world tailored for you."

"Or I for it," Sandy murmured, recalling not the opulent parties in the star-chambered ballroom, but instead, the fickle attentions of his parents, his father's cold smile.

"You were raised for it, then?" Peregrine asked. "To live in this secret world?"

"In a manner of speaking." Sandy had barely existed to his parents—even Reginald the heir had barely existed to them—because their mother lived for the Second Kingdom and its delights, and their father cared only for his manipulations and schemes. But Sandy had existed more than enough to his godparents, the gentle Foscourts, who'd practically adopted him. He'd spent every moment he could at Kelstone with them and their daughter Juliana, and when he was old enough, it was from them that he learned how the Second Kingdom should be. How it used to be before his father took over.

And then Reginald after him.

"There's more than living in the Second Kingdom for a Dartham, you see. The Duke of Jarrell is the head. The ruler."

"Reginald," Peregrine said. It wasn't a question.

"Yes, Reginald. He is the duke, and so the Second Kingdom is his. Fortunately, the Kingdom's members are all over the island, and there are plenty of revels held where he's not present. And so, I spend my time in London whenever I can help it, only returning when it would cause a scandal for me not to."

Sandy didn't mention that he'd all but fled to London once his education had been finished, desperate to leave behind the messy, poisonous atmosphere his parents had created and which Reginald had perpetuated. Sandy had thought that in London—and at court, no less—he'd find more people like the Foscourts, who were unbound from convention, but friendly and steady too. He could almost laugh at the absurdity of that younger Sandy if it didn't make him so depressed to remember it.

"But . . . ?" Peregrine prompted.

"How do you know there's a but?"

Peregrine just looked at him, and Sandy gave a sigh. "Yes, fine. There is a *but*. I stay away and partake mainly of the Kingdom's pleasures outside of my brother's purview, *but* sometimes I feel so restless and unhappy that I can't stand it. And sometimes that restlessness feels like homesickness."

"You miss Far Hope."

"I don't miss Far Hope as it is," Sandy clarified. "It's almost like I'm homesick for a Far Hope that doesn't exist. For the Far Hope that lives only in my mind."

"Why doesn't it exist?" Peregrine asked, sounding genuinely curious. "What's the difference between the kingdom where there's no law but pleasure and the kingdom in your mind?"

"What else?" Sandy responded. "*Who* else? Reginald. He is a shadow that covers everything."

Peregrine seemed to think about how he wanted to phrase his next question. "You say there's no limit in the Second Kingdom but acquiescence. Has he violated that limit?"

"Among the members? No, not that I know of. But with Reginald, anyone who isn't a member of the Second Kingdom, or fantastically wealthy, isn't a person to him and doesn't merit a limit."

There had been a relation of Reginald's wife who'd come to stay after her father's death, a girl who came with a profitable mill and water rights—so long as she was married off to someone willing to cede those rights to Reginald in exchange for a well-connected bride. The relation, Lydia, hadn't wanted the marriage, had fought against it until the duchess had locked her in her room to keep her from running. She'd run anyway. Sandy had been at Oxford at the time, and so he'd only heard the tale from the servants once he'd returned for that year's Michaelmas.

No, there'd been no limit of acquiescence for Lydia. Nor concern after she'd fled. Only spittle-flecked tirades about what Reginald would do if he ever caught her, and the occasional gloating over the mill, which had stayed in Reginald and Judith's ownership after the girl's disappearance.

Then there were the enclosures, which he'd only learned of last year—again from the servants. Sandy very much doubted the farmers and cottagers around Far Hope had acquiesced to having their livelihoods taken away.

"The Kingdom is supposed to be about pleasure above all —a place where vice is celebrated. But *good* vice, do you understand? Openness instead of narrowness. Liberality instead of restriction. But Reginald only sees the Kingdom as another way to increase his wealth and his power. He can't be as ruthless with the members as he is with everyone else, but it doesn't stop him from finding other ways to achieve his end of getting ever and ever richer. His machinations taint everything in the Kingdom."

"And the other people in the Kingdom? Do they feel the same as you? Is there no way to . . . remove him from his role?"

Sandy cocked an eyebrow. "What are you, a Leveller? No,

he is the duke, and the duke is the head of the kingdom. It's always been that way."

"Perhaps it could be a new way." Peregrine studied him. "Except you mentioned earlier that you didn't want to be the duke. I take that to mean you don't want to be the ruler of the Second Kingdom either?"

Sandy didn't answer at first, his mind flashing through the responsibilities, the burdens, the poisoned wells big and small that Reginald left everywhere he went. And as Sandy cataloged the work Reginald's successor would have to do, he idly ran his palm over his captor's lightly furred chest and stomach. Peregrine had a tall, broad frame, but despite his powerful shoulders and thighs, there was a spareness to him to spoke of a life without rest or luxury, and Sandy wondered again what had set him on this path, why he'd chosen this desperate vocation.

And for the first time that he could ever remember in his petted and pampered life, Sandy itched to take care of someone else. He felt it like a catch in his breath, like an ache in his bones. He wanted to feed this man until his lean frame filled and thickened. He wanted to make Peregrine sleep enough and eat enough—and fuck until all the tension was bled from his limbs.

He wanted Peregrine's grim heart in his hands, and he wanted to treasure it forever.

A stupid wish.

"I don't," Sandy said after a long a time. "I'm—I think I'm—"

He drew in a breath. Even after thinking about how he wanted to answer, he found the words hard to say. "I'm scared. Of it."

Peregrine didn't give him a look of disgust or of disbelief; he didn't prompt Sandy to say more. Instead, he waited patiently while Sandy pressed his face into the highwayman's warm shoulder and spoke the words against his skin.

"I don't have many virtues, but I do have these: I've never forced anyone into a decision they didn't want to make, and I've never defrauded someone who couldn't afford it. I've wheedled and whined and coaxed and flirted, but I've never locked someone in a room until they married whom I wanted them to marry. I've never used my position and influence to coerce someone poor and scared into my bed."

Peregrine stiffened under Sandy, but before Sandy could think too much of it, Peregrine was shifting so that he could wrap his arms around him. The warmth that tickled through Sandy's chest at this gesture was ridiculous. Who felt flattered by being held by a lover? And how could this small thing outweigh the fact that Peregrine was going to kill him?

But for the moment, it did. He relaxed into Peregrine's arms, rooting against the older man's muscled shoulder until he was totally comfortable.

Once he'd finally settled in, Peregrine asked, "Are you worried that if you'd become like Reginald if you were the duke?"

Like Reginald . . . like his father and mother . . .

Sandy had gone to London thinking he would finally be done with all the noisome games and fleeting affairs which filled the days of Reginald's denizens, and instead, he'd been drawn into just as many games, just as many affairs, all of them as noisome and fleeting. Perhaps he wasn't a villain like Reginald yet, but he'd hardly acquitted himself as a saint at court. Who knows what he'd be like with enough power, enough vipers whispering in his ear?

"Yes, of course I'm worried about that," Sandy said with a sigh. "Wouldn't you be? If your own natural virtues were so few to begin with?"

"I'm a highwayman," Peregrine reminded him. "My natural virtues are very few."

"I don't believe it," Sandy said, running a hand over Peregrine's stomach again. "I think you have some tragic, noble reason for taking to the road."

Peregrine didn't answer, but Sandy felt a new tension beneath his hand, something like stillness. Indecision, maybe.

He tilted his head up to look at the man holding him. This close, Sandy could see the dark grains of stubble on Peregrine's jaw and the tiny white starburst of a scar near his temple. His lips were parted, revealing the blunt edges of the teeth which had scored Sandy's neck and chest just an hour ago.

He could also see a faint, barely perceptible struggle in the thief's eyes. It was almost invisible—one blink too many, one blink too long—but Sandy had watched enough card players weigh whether to keep playing to recognize it.

Sandy was too impatient, too *eager* for anything of Peregrine's, for anything of this man's history or heart. "You can tell me," he said quickly, knowing he was playing his own hand too fast even as he played it. "I want to hear all about that tragic, noble reason. I want to know what my brother did to you. I want to know everything about you."

For an instant, it looked like Peregrine was going to tell him. Like he was going to trust him. His lips parted, and his throat worked, and his brow furrowed as if with effort, and—

The instant passed. Peregrine's face slid into its usual stony chill, and he efficiently disentangled himself from Sandy.

"Peregrine," Sandy said as the highwayman stood and walked to where his clothes were draped over a chair. "Stay at least. You don't have to talk. But stay."

"No."

Sandy's hands fisted on the bed. He hated being dismissed like this, and more than that, he hated that he'd told Peregrine things he'd only ever told Juliana, and now Peregrine wouldn't even *look* at him.

And—and—he didn't want Peregrine to leave. Sandy was

already cold without him, and the highwayman was better than warm; he was solid. Steady.

He made Sandy feel steadier just by being nearby.

Peregrine stepped into his breeches, not looking at Sandy. "You should sleep."

"*You* should sleep. Here. With me."

"I'll be outside," he replied. "In case you were thinking of escaping."

"I'm always thinking of escaping," Sandy said, annoyed now.

Peregrine didn't bother to respond. He left Sandy the candle, and Sandy stared at the dancing flame for a long time after his captor left, acutely aware of how ridiculous it was to cry over a lover's abrupt exit when the lover was his future murderer.

Sandy did it anyway.

Seven

PEREGRINE

"IS THERE a reason I'm not tied up?" Alexander demanded from the doorway of the sacristy.

It was late morning, and Peregrine was tired, having spent a sleepless night on the hard stone floor outside Alexander's cell, wishing viciously that he was back inside it with a sleeping Alexander clinging to him like a limpet. But he'd had no choice. He'd come so perilously close to telling Alexander things that he'd told no one, not even Lyd, and that wasn't right, that couldn't be right, could it? That this man he was supposed to kill—or at the very least, hate—was the only person he wanted to trust with memories so painful he barely trusted *himself* with them?

No, he'd been right to leave.

Except he'd been restless all night and was miserable today, and seeing Sandy barefoot and looking like some kind of fairy-tale prince somehow made everything better and worse at the same time.

"I must be the luckiest kidnapper ever," Peregrine said. "My captive *reminds* me to keep him bound."

"It's a favor to me, really," Alexander said. "And you owe me so many favors by now."

Peregrine grunted in response.

Alexander padded across the stone floor to the table where Peregrine sat. But he didn't take a chair for himself; instead, he hopped onto the table in front of Peregrine, sitting on his papers.

Peregrine wanted to be irritated, but it was difficult when Alexander's legs were spread so wide, and when his loose shirt had pulled to the side, exposing a bronze-pink nipple . . .

"Where are the others?" Alexander asked, reaching out to run his fingertips along the edge of Peregrine's jaw. It felt so good, so comforting, that Peregrine found himself allowing the touch, even though he shouldn't.

"They went to wait for the duchess on the road."

"Judith," Alexander said, sighing. "There's no love lost between us, but you don't suppose they'll hurt her, do you?"

Peregrine shook his head that he didn't know, his eyelids beginning to close as Alexander kept petting him. He couldn't remember ever being touched like this, with such affection. With no further purpose other than to touch.

"I'm not sure how far Lyd will go, but if I had my guess, I'd say she won't hurt the duchess. Not badly, at least. I did think they'd be back by now, though."

Alexander made a thinking noise. "Judith was feeling poorly when I left two days ago. Maybe she'd planned to leave but then hadn't felt up to it."

Peregrine nodded, eyes fully closed now. This was ludicrous, foolish beyond all reason, being stroked into submission like a lazy lion by clever prey. But neither could he bring himself to stop it. Last night with Alexander had been the most sharply exhilarating pleasure he'd ever known, but this moment, with his captive perched insouciantly on the table and his caresses sweet on Peregrine's face . . .

This was the kind of moment men fought wars for.

* * *

PEREGRINE SPENT the rest of the morning readying baths for each of them, and then after they washed, Peregrine bound Alexander's wrists as he had yesterday. Alexander's cock was thickly visible in his breeches before Peregrine finished wrapping even a single wrist with silk, and Peregrine's pulse sped as he thought about what might happen later, after several hours of keeping Alexander so thoroughly teased.

But despite the pleasant, if petulant, scenery of his day, Peregrine began to feel the slightest curl of concern for Lyd and the others as the sun moved across the sky. It wasn't a true worry, because Lyd was very good at her chosen vocation, and Ned and the rest were the perfect companions for highway robbery, but it was the seed of a worry. They had left witnesses to Alexander's abduction, after all, which meant there was a chance that there would be a reward already posted for their band's capture.

Which meant people would be scouring the road for traces of Peregrine and his fellow thieves even more than they usually were.

Peregrine decided to check the old alms box at the front of the priory, which was where the band left each other notes, and where any messengers from Chagford or beyond left their messages as well. Peregrine was careful only to hire people he knew he could trust, but even so, the messengers believed the priory was a waypoint for Peregrine and his thieves, a convenient place to stable horses or wait out some rain, and not their true hideout. He trusted those he hired, but even good men could be tempted by the thought of unprotected loot.

Or a handsome reward.

"I'm going outside for a few moments," he told Alexander, who was currently lying on his stomach, reading one of the books Peregrine had found for him. "Do I need to tie you down so you don't leave your bed?"

"Only my bed has this edition of the Earl of Rochester's poetry, so no," Alexander said, not taking his eyes off the book, kicking his feet in the air like a schoolboy as he read. "But leave my wrists tied, if you please."

"As you say," Peregrine said and left his pretty captive on the bed.

Peregrine quickly checked on the horses and then scouted the front of the priory to make sure there was no one about. Assured that it was only him, Alexander, and the horses nearby, he went to the box, which indeed had a small note tucked under the lid.

He replaced the note with a few shillings for the next person delivering a message, and then he ducked under the crumbling beams of the priory's entry and strode back inside, unfolding the note and reading it as he went.

He stopped.

It wasn't an update about constables or magistrates or rewards. It wasn't even a message from Lyd and the others.

It was a message from the duke.

He'd agreed to pay the ransom.

Peregrine stared at the note for another moment longer, stared until the words blurred into the shadows gathering in the creases of the paper.

I wanted this.

This is what I wanted.

It had seemed so genius when Alexander had suggested it —not only revenge, but revenge unfolded, layered over itself, plague on top of famine on top of fire. Loss, then grief, then death.

Peregrine could make the duke suffer as Peregrine himself suffered, and then when the opportunity arose again, he would kill the duke, and, at long last, the emptiness inside Peregrine would be filled. At long last, his heart would stop its seething, aching *lack*, and his world would feel right again, as it hadn't since the day he'd kissed his mother and siblings goodbye and left to join the army.

So why didn't he feel victorious right now? Why didn't he rush to pen a reply, to strategize how much more of a ransom he could negotiate the duke into paying?

Because you know it's the beginning of the end for Alexander.

The Darthams were selfish, cruel, rapacious, *evil*—the thought of them made Peregrine sick. But though he'd once hated the idea of Alexander Dartham, he didn't hate the reality of Alexander at all.

Not in the slightest.

And the thought of any kind of harm coming to the barefoot rake currently lounging on his bed and reading—the rake who was half courage, half insolence, all spoiled—made Peregrine feel like he couldn't breathe.

He'd been tying Alexander's wrists with silk because it bothered him to think of Alexander's skin being scratched by proper rope—did he really think he could kill Alexander? *Truly?* But then what did that mean about Peregrine, about his pledge to destroy the Dartham family, either through ruin or death?

What if . . . what if he could have both? Revenge without hurting Alexander?

I'm not going to set you free.

Maybe you'll decide to keep me instead, Alexander had teased.

Peregrine folded the note, his thoughts racing, his mind turning over every possible solution. It would still be a blow for the duke if Peregrine took the ransom but didn't return the ransomed heir. Perhaps Peregrine could even spread the word that he *had* killed Alexander, and all the while, Alexander would be tucked away in the priory, reading books and complaining about the wine.

The image of Alexander remaining here, staying a petulant and handsome thorn in Peregrine's side, eased the tension in his chest. His pulse slowed.

Yes, yes, that was what he would do. He'd demand the ransom but keep Alexander alive. He'd have revenge *and* his rake.

His rake. He liked how those words felt in his mind . . . like a soft breeze on a summer's night. Like a kiss in the dark.

Alexander could be his. Revenge could be his.

All of it could be his.

When he finally reached the sanctuary, he barely stopped. He dropped the note on top of his papers as he passed by the table, took something else off the dinner table nearby, and strode straight to the sacristy, where Alexander had rolled onto his back and had the book propped against his raised knees as he read. Peregrine set down the small bottle he'd brought from the sanctuary and stalked over to the bed, taking the book off Alexander's stomach and tossing it onto the mattress. He untied the rake's wrists quickly, easily, letting the silk unravel into soft coils next to Alexander's ribs.

Alexander blinked up at him, his dark eyes catching the light of the candles burning nearby.

Black and blue and gold, glittering and glittering.

"Have you come to see if I can do it?" Alexander asked softly.

Peregrine pulled off his shirt and started on his breeches. "Do what?"

"Seduce my way to freedom."

Peregrine stared at the young man on his bed. He couldn't know about the note Peregrine had just received, could he? No. No, he wouldn't have known where to look for it in the alms box to begin with, and Peregrine knew he'd betrayed nothing when he'd walked in. Nothing other than grim lust, of course.

When Peregrine didn't answer, Alexander's full mouth curled in a smile so devious that Peregrine was certain half of London had lost their hearts or purses or both to it. What a highwayman Alexander Dartham would have made—he would've ridden up to a carriage and smiled that smile and the occupants would have showered him with jewels just for being so beautiful and captivating.

Just for being so very, very wonderful.

"I seem to remember telling you that I'm always willing to try the seduction route of escape," Alexander murmured. He didn't sit up, but rather stretched like a spoiled cat in the sun, and then his hands went to his waist, where he began playing idly with the fabric of his shirt, drawing it up higher and higher until Peregrine could see the delectable well of his navel.

"What if it doesn't work?" Peregrine asked, his voice gone a little rough as he finished undressing and mounted the bed again, this time with both knees so he could crawl over Alexander, who was still smiling to himself like he was about to swindle an entire table of courtiers playing cards.

"Then I suppose," Alexander said sweetly, sliding his hands up and around Peregrine's neck, "I shall have to keep trying. You wouldn't mind that, would you? If I had to practice a few times in order to get the seduction just right?"

"It's already just right," Peregrine heard himself say.

The truth tasted sharp and sweet on his tongue as he added hoarsely, "*You're* just right."

Alexander's smile faded, and his eyebrows drew together.

He looked confused, like Peregrine wasn't playing the game which Alexander had been planning to cheat at.

"Peregrine," he said, hesitantly, but Peregrine didn't think he'd be able to answer any question that came next, and so he kissed Alexander before Alexander could say anything more.

Alexander's grasp tightened on Peregrine's neck, and then his fingers were sliding into Peregrine's hair, rumpling it, tugging at it, until he finally found the ribbon tying Peregrine's queue and pulled it free. His hair tumbled around their faces like a curtain, shutting out the light from the candles and from the fire, and in that private darkness, Peregrine licked past Alexander's mouth until he could feel the sweet silk of Alexander's tongue against his.

As Peregrine kissed him, he braced on one arm and used his free hand to find the jut of Alexander's hip, then the curve of his backside. He gripped and squeezed there and then pressed them together where it mattered most. The broadcloth of Alexander's breeches was a little rough against Peregrine's cock, but the roughness felt good as he moved his hips against the other man; it had him panting after only a few thrusts.

He couldn't remember being this wound up, not even as a lad sneaking into the barn with a shepherd for the first time. He couldn't remember ever having his body pressed against someone's like this, kissing and simply *feeling*. As a soldier, any encounter had been necessarily brief and efficient. Impersonal.

But with Alexander, everything was languorous, lingering, indulgent—not merely relieving a physical need, but savoring something wonderful.

"How would you seduce me?" Peregrine breathed between kisses.

"So you admit now it's a possibility that I can?" Alexander murmured.

Peregrine could feel Alexander's mouth curving against

his, and then he smiled himself. "You're awfully smug for a captive."

"Obviously, I'm smug." Alexander reached between them, and his fingertips ghosted across the corners of Peregrine's mouth. "I made the terror of the Queen's roads *smile*. And I haven't even touched his cock yet."

You've only touched everything else. His thoughts, his heart, even the faint wisps of what could be called a soul—Alexander's fingertips had brushed over them all. And Peregrine didn't know how he felt about it . . .

Only that he wasn't ready for it to stop.

"But a smile is still a long way from seduction," Alexander continued. "*Hmm.* What shall I do to win my freedom? How should I seduce such a stern"—his fingers dropped to Peregrine's bare chest, and then skated down his sides, making him shiver—"ferocious"—then his fingers tickled over Peregrine's hips and Peregrine huffed out a laugh that made the rake's evil grin spread even wider—"stoic man?"

"If you keep insulting my dignity like this, I may have to return you to your bindings," Peregrine threatened, nuzzling against Alexander's neck and inhaling the scent there. It smelled like soap and somehow still like *Alexander*—citrus and spice.

"Oh dear," said Alexander. "Oh no. Whatever shall I do."

"You could get back to seducing me properly," Peregrine suggested. He kissed Alexander's neck and then levered himself up to look down at the younger man spread underneath him. Alexander's near-black hair was in a halo of dark silk, and his already full mouth was swollen with kissing. Without breaking their gaze, Alexander slowly, carefully stripped himself out of his clothes. Peregrine eased up so his captive could pull them all the way off, and then he lowered his hips to Alexander's once he was finished undressing so that naked flesh could touch naked flesh.

Peregrine grunted in pleasure, and Alexander's gaze grew flirtatious.

"Would you like me like this?" Alexander murmured coyly, spreading his thighs even wider under Peregrine and putting his hands against Peregrine's chest. "Like a virgin? Like I don't know how good it will feel? Like I can only tremble underneath you while you show me?"

Peregrine's cock surged against Alexander's stomach, answering for him.

"Or . . . ," Alexander said, seeming to have an idea. His eyes moved past Peregrine to the closed door, and there was an icy stab of fear that his prisoner would bolt for the door while Peregrine was hazed over with lust. But then he realized that even Alexander wasn't reckless enough to plunge into the chilly moors completely naked, and also that Alexander was looking at the edge of the table instead, where Peregrine had set a small bottle of oil.

With surprising strength, Alexander flipped Peregrine onto his back. He tossed his hair over his shoulder and gave him a triumphant grin before sliding off the bed, sauntering over to the table, and getting the bottle.

Peregrine's blood was already hot enough to simmer, but watching the Dartham heir move around utterly naked with that fluid grace of his made Peregrine feel like his very skin was about to catch fire. Alexander's mussed hair waved over his shoulders, his nipples were pulled into tight points, and the small nip in his waist was so very visible like this, just waiting for Peregrine's hands. And Alexander's cock—pointed to by a narrow, elegant trail of dark hair—was beyond tempting. Straight and veined and as lovely as something carved from marble by a deeply skilled hand.

Peregrine wanted to put it in his mouth.

"Or you could be the virgin," Alexander said as he came

back to the bed and climbed gracefully onto the mattress. "Would you like that? If you trembled beneath me instead?"

"What would *you* like?"

Alexander's expression shuttered and he looked away for a moment, ostensibly down to the bottle to open it. When he looked back up, his expression was the same blithe one as earlier. "I like whatever will seduce you the best, of course," he said smoothly. "Now give me your hand, please."

Peregrine hesitated. He wanted to know what Alexander had been thinking—what Alexander *wanted*—but even wondering felt ridiculous because what else would Alexander want? To be free of Peregrine and safely back to his life, of course.

Peregrine nearly opened his mouth to reassure Alexander that he wasn't planning to hurt him any longer . . . but then he couldn't bring himself to utter anything at all. Not because he didn't want Alexander to know that he was safe, but because he didn't want to bring up the subject in the first place. He was ashamed, maybe, of having ever wanted to kill Alexander at all.

Ashamed that he still didn't plan on setting Alexander free.

In any case, Alexander distracted Peregrine beyond all thought. He took Peregrine's hand in his own and then gently, carefully, drizzled oil over the first two fingers, giving Peregrine a smoldering look as he did. Peregrine's pulse kicked.

"Work me open," Alexander said, his own racing pulse obvious in the thrumming at the side of his throat. In the erratic bob and swell of the pretty cock between his thighs. "Make me ready."

And then he turned and presented himself to Peregrine.

Peregrine couldn't stop the groan that tore out of his chest at the sight. Alexander was beautiful everywhere, even in the secret places where his body opened to take a lover, and the sight of that beauty nearly undid Peregrine. His hand shaking, he reached up and grazed a single fingertip over the sensitive flesh on offer.

Alexander let out a puff of air that was almost a sigh, as if he were both relieved and excited by the touch.

Peregrine knew neither of them were virgins or seducers; he could push them to any pace, and Alexander would be right there with him. But he didn't want to push. He didn't want this to be fast, mechanical.

Forgettable.

He suddenly wanted to be all over Alexander in the same way Alexander was all over him—to touch Alexander's thoughts and his heart and his soul. Peregrine didn't know if he could do that merely from making love—he'd never tried and no one had ever tried with him—but that was what he wanted, and so that was what he would do.

He grazed over the pleated skin again as his other hand slid up Alexander's lean thigh and caressed the smooth cheek of his backside. He kept stroking that firm curve as he swirled his fingertip against Alexander's entrance and made everything sweet and slick in the process. It wasn't long before there were goose bumps all over the rake's skin, along his back and thighs and arse.

Peregrine loved feeling those goose bumps, this proof that he, who'd done nothing but the briskest and most trans-actional kinds of lovemaking, had the power to affect a seasoned libertine like Lord Alexander Dartham. He sanded his free hand over Alexander's skin and whispered, "Breathe."

Alexander breathed. Peregrine pushed.

There was enough oil to make passage easy, if something as searing and squeezing as this could be called *easy*. Peregrine's mind filled with images of him surging to his knees behind Alexander and taking him in one rough thrust—pushing

Alexander to his stomach and mounting him—yanking him off the bed and bending him over and—

But Peregrine wanted this instead. This slow, stroking invasion that made Alexander shiver and shiver and shiver until he seemed to be nothing but panting and goose bumps, until Peregrine could see between his legs the wet spot Alexander's cock was leaving on the coverlet as clear seed leaked from the tip.

"Stroke yourself," Peregrine said, gently working his finger until he could find that swollen spot inside. Alexander let out a gasp, and then his hand flew to his organ, which he rubbed furiously, almost clumsily, his libertine's grace leaving him as Peregrine continued to caress the gland inside his body.

Peregrine found the bottle propped against a nearby pillow and added more oil, and then slid a second finger inside Alexander, which earned him a noise so guttural and yet so heavenly that Peregrine couldn't wait to hear it again. He stroked inside with two fingers now, until Alexander began moving against him, shamelessly fucking himself against the highwayman's touch.

And then Peregrine knew what he wanted, how he wanted to be seduced.

He wanted to be seduced purely by watching Alexander like this, with Alexander urgent and near helpless with how good he felt.

Peregrine slid his hand free and then pulled at Alexander's hips until the rake turned to blink at him. His cheeks and chest were flushed; his cock stuck straight out like a blunt sword. His lips were parted, and his brows were pulled together in an expression of utter bewilderment, as if he couldn't imagine *why* Peregrine would do something so awful as to stop.

"I want you on top," Peregrine murmured, already pulling

Alexander over him. "I want you to make yourself come on me."

Alexander gave a little shudder, his ribs jerking with fast, tattered breaths. "Are you sure—I'm not the one being —seduced?"

Peregrine's only answer was a smile; he relished how Alexander's usual coquettish demeanor was falling apart right now—the way his eyes roved hungrily over Peregrine's body as he positioned himself to fuck—the way his tongue darted out to his lower lip in concentration as he guided Peregrine past that first slick barrier into the searing forge beyond. The way he unselfconsciously shook his hair out of his face and then gave a soft whine as he impaled himself.

Peregrine gentled his hands up and down Alexander's thighs, making soothing noises as Alexander pushed down, even as he himself had to lock every muscle in his stomach and thighs to keep from surging up into the snug velvet of Alexander's body.

His patience was rewarded, however, as Alexander fully seated himself and then gave a tentative rock forward. Another one of those heavenly noises left him, and he gave Peregrine a look of dazed helplessness.

"Good?" Peregrine asked. His voice was rough, hoarse, and his entire body was shaking with the restraint it took to let Alexander squirm and writhe on top of him, to let the Dartham lord find the right angle, the right movements.

"Yes," Alexander breathed, his eyelids fluttering. "More than good. I've never—it's never been like this before."

"You on top?" Peregrine asked.

"No," Alexander said, his mouth hooking ruefully to the side. "Never with someone patient on the bottom. One moment—oh. *Oh.*" He seemed to have found just the right way to move, and he did it again, his erection dragging along

Peregrine's abdomen and making him release another puff of air. Another *oh.*

Peregrine tried to focus on one thing, any one thing, to keep his building climax at bay, but it was impossible. Even aside from Alexander's body gripping him like a hot glove, from the sweet sensation of Alexander's cock rubbing against Peregrine's stomach, there was the *sight* of him. The slender hips, the dark hair tumbling everywhere, his face in an expression of surprised ecstasy, as if he hadn't expected it to feel as good as it did.

It made Peregrine wonder how selfish Alexander's past lovers had been, that it was a revelation for him to be able to take his time, to put his own pleasure first.

"Spend for me," Peregrine said, sliding his hands up to Alexander's hips and then up to his waist. "I want to see you."

"I think that's—normally—the seducer's line—" Alexander panted, but he braced his hands and Peregrine's chest and began riding Peregrine for all he was worth, choosing the speed and the angle and the depth. Each rock of his hips tightened the grip his body had on Peregrine's cock; each rock meant that his secret place stroked Peregrine with a slippery, viselike heat. It drew his orgasm closer; it pulled his bollocks tight to his body; it had his hips restless underneath Alexander's.

"Oh, Peregrine," Alexander said, his breaths all sounding like gasps now, all of them desperate. "I'm—it's—"

He didn't have to announce it. His prick swelled even more on top of Peregrine's stomach, and with a low cry, his hips gave a series of quick, arrhythmic thrusts. Peregrine was entranced by the sight of that beautiful organ swelling and then throbbing out jet after jet of white seed, loving the visible proof of the rake's satisfaction spilled all over his skin.

Alexander's hips stilled and his head dropped between his shoulders as he panted and quivered his way through the aftershocks. Peregrine somehow managed to hold on, to fight back the tide of his own need to spend, until Alexander was finished.

After he'd settled, the younger man peeped up through a glossy lock of hair that had tumbled over one eye and said, "Some highwayman you are. Aren't you supposed to be all about plunder and theft? What have you taken for yourself right now? Nothing. You're more rector than robber, I think."

Peregrine laughed. "I can plunder more, if you'd like."

Alexander gave him a coy look from behind his hair. "Will you show me how the soldiers do it?"

"Maybe another time," Peregrine said. "The soldier's way is hardly a seduction."

"I'll confess a secret to you, Peregrine Hind. You don't have to seduce me. If you'd like to take me like a soldier would . . . " Alexander shivered again, his sated cock stirring against Peregrine's stomach. "I have no objections."

Neither did Peregrine. If he somehow managed to steal more time with this man, he would want all kinds of lovemaking. Slow and fast, rough and whatever this had been too—not gentle maybe, and certainly not sweet, but the kind of sex where selfishness was transformed into something fantastic. Where one lover's pleasure spun a silken web around them both, where taking was also giving.

"For now," Peregrine said, "I'll take you like a highwayman." He was already pulling out, moving. Pushing the rake onto his back, and then onto his stomach, which meant his firm backside was there for Peregrine to spread and penetrate once more.

He came into Alexander with a deliberate but inexorable thrust, and then once he'd fully mounted his captive, he started fucking in earnest, with quick, rough strokes that had them both groaning together. As he rutted, he watched Alexander's slender fingers twisting in the covers; he watched as Alexander reached underneath himself and desperately handled his cock.

The orgasm wasn't only in Peregrine's prick, but in his stomach and chest and thighs too, and it thudded through his blood like the drums of war. With a ragged grunt and a surge of his hips, Peregrine's climax roiled its way up his shaft and then released torrent after torrent into Alexander's pliant, waiting heat.

Peregrine kept riding his wonderful flirt of prisoner through it all, determined to pump everything into the man in front of him. Sinuous shudders racked Alexander's body as he came for a second time, and Peregrine caught the quick movements of the rake's hand as he finished milking his orgasm free.

There was no bliss like this, no satisfaction that matched pulling out and seeing his seed dripping free of this beautiful man's body, and then rolling his lover over to see the slick mess he'd made while he'd been receiving Peregrine's pleasure.

Peregrine suddenly wanted never to leave the priory again. He only wanted this, day after day. Alexander Dartham, frolicsome and spoiled and safe.

With him.

It would be worth giving up the road for, it could even be worth giving up revenge for, but for the first time in years, Peregrine didn't want to think about revenge at all.

Stunned by that realization, and a little panicked by it too, he tidied up the mess they made and then pulled the rake tightly into his arms, trying to breathe past the sudden swell of emotion.

How could it be that this libertine, this *Dartham*, had become more important to him than the need for vengeance and justice for innocent lives? How could the mere thought of Alexander being hurt by him make Peregrine feel like he'd been torn open by cannon fire?

After only a few short days?

Peregrine didn't know the answer. He'd walked into this room so certain of his future, so confident in his solution, but perversely, he felt like he knew himself less after losing himself inside Alexander. Like he was slowly dissolving, and the only thing keeping him whole was the warm lover lying dozily in his arms.

Eight

SANDY

PEREGRINE HIND, ex-soldier, present-day kidnapper, and Terror of the Queen's Roads, snored. Rather adorably.

Sandy looked up at the man whose chest he was currently using as a pillow and couldn't help the grin on his face. He'd never fucked like that, not once. Oh sure, he'd tried every position and sex act under the sun, but never had a partner allowed the use of their body for *Sandy's* pleasure. Never had a partner waited patiently while Sandy learned what felt good, what he wanted, and then waited even more patiently as Sandy chased down a cataclysm that was more potent for the time it took to seek it out. Pleasure at Oxford—and then in the Second Kingdom once Sandy had been initiated at the age of twenty-one—had been a game, and the rules of the game were simple: if one cared too much, then one lost.

So he'd pretended not to care. He'd pretended that he was as jaded as the rest, because the alternative was either to abstain altogether or to take the way other people took—not without consent necessarily, but without concern—and he couldn't make himself do that. Perhaps it was the influence of the Foscourts, or maybe the memories of his own parents' selfishness, but he found he couldn't use someone for pleasure unless he knew the using was at least mutual. Not that he hadn't enjoyed the mutual using; he'd enjoyed it plenty! But tonight had been like discovering a new room in a house he'd always known, or a new chapter in his favorite book.

It had been a gift.

And wonder of wonders, he'd also somehow made this highwayman smile—and *laugh*. He'd seen the heat and the affection sparkling in Peregrine's silver eyes, and it had been an epiphany, a vision. He doubted Peregrine Hind would ever be a joyful man—or even an easy one—but seeing the gradual thawing of the highwayman for *him*, for Sandy Dartham, was powerfully alluring, to say the least.

Sandy watched Peregrine sleep for a few more minutes, enjoying the way those stern features softened in repose— enjoying how, even in sleep, Peregrine's arm clasped Sandy tightly to him. It was a possessive gesture, dominant and greedy, and Sandy loved how it felt so much that he could have stayed nestled there for the rest of the month. But when his stomach started growling with hunger, he slipped from the bed to hunt down something to eat.

The others still hadn't returned from their attempt to rob the duchess, and so Sandy padded out in his breeches and nothing else, shivering a little at the cool air of the sanctuary after being curled against a warm thief for so long. He poked around the table, tearing off a piece of bread and chewing on it as he wondered how the other robbers were getting on with Judith and how Judith was faring. She was a cruel woman— she and Reginald were very well matched in that respect—but she had been doing poorly when they'd stayed over in Exeter during their trip from London, and Sandy had felt bad for her. There was nothing worse than traveling while sick, and no cure for it except to get home as fast as possible; he'd even arranged for an extra coach so that she and her maid could ride in more comfort without him crowding the seat.

Still eating his bread, Sandy wandered over to the table where Peregrine sometimes sat to do his work. Funny that robbery had the same endless stacks of paper running a dukedom had. Some of it must have been correspondences, Sandy supposed, with fences and innkeepers like the one in Exeter who'd informed the band about the duchess. He unfolded the paper on top, more out of idle curiosity than anything else.

And then.

And then he saw.

> *duke to pay one thousand in coin.*
> *arrange place for payment and handing over the lord*
> *alexander?*
> *post response by dawn tomorrow.*
>
> *-x*

Sandy sat in the chair, stunned. Not *surprised*, certainly, he'd known that Reginald would ransom him—although one thousand pounds was so far beneath what Sandy had estimated his own worth to be that he was a little offended—but he supposed he hadn't considered the ransoming would happen this quickly. He'd thought that he'd have more time to escape, or to woo his freedom from his captor, or . . .

Or more time to stare into your captor's exquisite silver eyes while he fucks you into a bone-shaking climax.

Sandy stared at the note, his mind twisted up around his thoughts, his chest feeling all twisted up too. He'd somehow forgotten what it had felt like to be on his knees, watching Peregrine's finger curl over the trigger of a pistol. He'd forgotten that he *had* to escape, and escape quickly, because

Peregrine was planning to kill him the moment Reginald handed over the ransom.

He'd forgotten because Peregrine made it impossible to remember.

Sandy swore at himself as he got to his feet. He knew better than to let a pretty face distract him—he knew because ordinarily, *he* was the pretty face doing the distracting. And that Peregrine's face wasn't pretty was beyond the point. He was lovely the same way the moors and hills around Far Hope were lovely, with a kind of lonely, elemental beauty. He fucked Sandy like Sandy had never been fucked before—not as a convenient playmate or as the means to an end, but like Sandy was the end itself. Like Sandy *mattered*.

And maybe it wasn't the beauty or the pleasure that had so arrested Sandy, but Peregrine's unflinching wholeness. Peregrine was, simply, honestly, *grimly* himself.

That, too, reminded Sandy of the hills around his childhood home. But that unflinching wholeness was the same reason Sandy needed to leave. Because Peregrine had never hidden that he was after revenge and revenge alone, and if Sandy had secretly hoped that his dimples and bed-play would endear the highwayman to him—at least enough to buy him his life—then it was time he admitted the enterprise had been a failure. Peregrine had said nothing about keeping him alive after the ransom, hadn't betrayed even a sliver of willingness to do so. His wordlessness in the face of this note, which he'd so obviously seen, proved it to Sandy.

His death was still part of the plan.

Sandy looked at the note again, suddenly feeling like an invisible hourglass had been turned over. Reginald could be mustering the money for the ransom right now; in fact, Sandy couldn't even be sure of when the highwayman had received the note. For all he knew, Peregrine had already arranged the ransom exchange, and Sandy was going to die tomorrow or the day after.

The reverie of being tied up and ravished into boneless pleasure was over. The cold truth had come to burn it away.

He had to run.

Now.

He set the note back where he found it, and he then went to the door of the sacristy to see if Peregrine was still soundly asleep.

He was, flat on his back and snoring softly, the sheets caught around his hips and one muscled thigh partially exposed. His lips were parted ever so slightly, his long eyelashes on his cheeks, his hair everywhere on the pillow. One arm rested exactly as it had been when Sandy had been snuggled next to him—as if, even while asleep, Peregrine was waiting for Sandy to return to bed.

Walking away from the man who was going to kill him was like being pressed with stones. Sandy could barely breathe as he did it, and each breath hurt something deep inside his chest as he dragged it in and then released it. He struggled to keep his inhales and exhales quiet as he crept to the corridor that led to the former monks' cells. Peregrine's was easy to find—it had only the essential things inside it, while the others were piled with finery and spoils. Sandy slipped inside.

He had grown up in this corner of Devonshire and knew quite well how forbidding any flight through it would be, which is why he didn't feel too guilty for taking Peregrine's extra pair of boots and a thick coat. From the sanctuary, he also took a small satchel with a flagon of water and some bread, a tinderbox, and then a wide-brimmed hat which looked like a relic from the Civil War.

Sandy considered stealing a horse, but the moment he approached the stables, there was a good deal of snorting and stomping and neighing, and he had the sudden terror the noise would wake Peregrine and scuttle his escape before he'd gotten to the lane leading out from the priory.

After taking an unlit torch from just inside the stable entrance, he backed away from the stables and then walked as quietly as he could through the dark yard to the lane. The moon was close to full, but clouds drifted over it now and again, and the world was reduced to rivers and pools of shadow. But Sandy wouldn't light the torch until he was very far from the priory, not if he could help it.

He kept looking over his shoulder, expecting Peregrine to be charging behind him on one of those noisy horses Sandy had been too timid to steal, but he never was. No one else was on the lane either, and when the lane joined to a slightly wider road, Sandy still had the route to himself—along with the occasional wild pony grazing nearby, which shuffled off whenever he got close.

Sandy breathed with relief as he turned onto the main thoroughfare, which was unoccupied but perhaps riskier, given its more exposed vantages. But it had the important benefit of being somewhat familiar. If that was the bridge he thought it was . . . and yes, if that was his favorite stone circle poking its teeth up into the moonlit sky . . . then he knew where he was. More importantly, he was perhaps only a few hours' hard walking from Far Hope. From safety.

So why didn't he feel relieved?

Because you're not there yet, Sandy told himself firmly. It couldn't be because he was regretting his flight away from Peregrine. It couldn't be because he *missed* Peregrine and being Peregrine's captive plaything. Sandy had grown up at Far Hope; he was a fully initiated citizen of the Second Kingdom, and he *knew* the difference between playing and real life.

He and Peregrine hadn't been playing a game of captivity. It had been real.

Unfortunately, everything else had been real too.

Ignoring the unhappiness that built and built inside him like a wave refusing to crest, Sandy marched on, trotting as fast as he could through the more visible areas of the road, going carefully through the hills and shadowy combes. By his reckoning, Peregrine's friends would be hunting Judith's coach some miles east of here, but he still couldn't take the chance of being found. And it was hardly like Peregrine Hind and his gang were the only thieves in Devonshire. While these moors were too remote and poorly traveled to attract the notice of most robbers, who could ever be sure? There was no point in escaping Peregrine only to die at the hands of someone else—someone who wouldn't even have moonlight eyes to soothe the unpleasantness of being murdered.

Ignoring the ache in his feet and the chill in his fingers, Sandy pressed on as fast as he could.

* * *

HE THOUGHT he might only be an hour away from Far Hope when he heard it.

Thunder. Thunder when he could look up and see the moon through the thin clouds, and the stars between them.

Someone was on the road and traveling fast.

Sandy reacted as quickly as he could, darting past a boulder and ducking, praying that the shadows would hide him, praying that it was only an ordinary traveler cantering down the road.

But of course, it was no ordinary traveler. When Sandy dared a peep over the edge of the boulder, he saw the huge black horse and the tall frame of Peregrine Hind. He had dropped down as quickly as he could, but when he heard the horse slowing as it approached, he knew he'd been sighted.

Peregrine had found him.

With a bolt of panic, Sandy surged to his feet and

attempted to plunge into the murky cut of a nearby brook, but it was no use. A cold hand clamped around his wrist and yanked him back, and then Sandy was pulled into a hard body, a hand coming tight on his jaw to tilt Sandy's face up to his pursuer's. The hat toppled off his head and fell behind him and was immediately forgotten.

"You can get on the horse willingly," Peregrine said, his voice shaking a little. "Or I can throw you over the saddle and walk you back. Which do you prefer?"

The moonlight was coming from behind Peregrine, and so Sandy couldn't read his expression, or even his eyes, which were no more than glimmers in the dark. But he could sense an implacable fury rolling off the highwayman in waves; he could hear the dangerous tremble in Peregrine's voice.

Sandy tried to think like he was playing a game of cards, like he was examining his own hand and reading the tells of the other players at the table. Except in this case, he couldn't bow out of a game gracefully if his cards were too poor to play. He could only keep betting and bluffing.

Or he could cheat.

Yes. He could cheat.

Sandy pulled away and started walking toward the horse, waiting by the saddle as Peregrine followed and gave him a look full of things Sandy couldn't properly parse. It was too dark. Peregrine mounted the horse easily, and then just as easily helped Sandy up behind him, settling Sandy onto the horse's back behind the saddle.

Peregrine turned his head and commanded, "Hold on," and then after Sandy slid his hands around Peregrine's waist, Peregrine urged the horse into a careful walk.

Sandy was already trying to decide how he'd cheat his way to freedom. Would he act contrite and attempt to elicit arousal or pity? Was he strong enough to hurt Peregrine or push him off the horse? Could he find a way to send word to Reginald once he got back to the priory—or maybe make sure the messenger got a forged note, telling Reginald that the exchange was no longer happening?

He was so wrapped up in his thoughts that he didn't notice the clapper bridge until they were clattering over it. A bridge that was very decidedly not on the way to the hideout.

"Wait," Sandy said after a moment. "We're not going back to the priory."

"Not tonight," Peregrine said. "A storm is moving in. It'll catch us before we make it back."

"So you're taking us deeper into the moors?" Sandy asked in a doubtful voice.

"No," came the low response. "There's shelter nearby."

Sandy sincerely doubted it, since they were still along the main road, and he knew there was nothing for another few miles until they reached the little parish village belonging to Far Hope. But Peregrine surprised him, and, after a mile or so, they turned onto a narrow lane bordered by low stone fences.

Though the light was still faint, Sandy could see the humps of white dotting the fields as they passed.

Sheep. Many of them.

Peregrine led them not to a shepherd's hut but to what appeared to be an abandoned longhouse—a thatched stone-built farmhouse joined to a barn at the far end. Shutters hung at crooked angles from the small windows, and the front door had a greenish film growing on the wood.

Peregrine helped Sandy dismount and then alighted from the horse himself, striding up to the door with no hesitation at all and pushing it open like he'd been there a thousand times before. Since it was the perfect kind of hiding place for a highwayman, maybe he had.

Sandy watched Peregrine's dark form disappear into the even darker house and weighed his chances of taking the horse and running, but Peregrine came back out before he could act.

"Come," the highwayman said. "Now."

Sandy followed him in, finding the highwayman already walking to the fireplace and getting to his knees as if to strike a fire. There was a stack of slender logs next to the hearth along with a small cauldron and a neat row of dried peat bricks; in front of the fireplace were two chairs and the frame for a cot.

It was rustic to be sure, but it looked like it was in regular use, and there were a few domestic touches deeper in the recesses of the house—a heavy Bible on a table, a spinning wheel, a small chair clearly built for a child. Sandy found it interesting that none of it had been burned. It would've certainly been more convenient to burn a chair or a spinning wheel than gather the scanty amounts of wood from around these parts, and it was hardly worth cutting and drying peat for a mere hideout.

The fire lit, Peregrine ducked out of the house again, and Sandy realized too late that he was walking the horse into the barn, because by the time Sandy decided this was his chance, Peregrine was rounding the corner and on his way back in. Even in the dark, Sandy could tell that the look Peregrine gave him was not an amused one, and Sandy slunk back inside.

Before he got to the fire, though, he felt that hand on his wrist again. He didn't know what he expected as he turned— anger, perhaps, or more unfeeling chill—but what he didn't expect was the unfiltered agony scrawled all over the highwayman's face, now visible in the dancing light of the fire.

Peregrine hauled Sandy against his chest, his arms tight around him and his hands roving everywhere—in Sandy's hair and along his back and even his backside—and then he pressed his face into Sandy's damp hair.

"Stay," the highwayman breathed. "Stay with me. Stay here."

"Obviously I have to stay here," Sandy muttered. "You dragged me here on your horse, remember?"

Peregrine ignored him, pulling back to cradle Sandy's face in his hands. "I was so worried," he said, his hands shaking against Sandy's cheek and jaw. "When I woke up and realized you'd gone . . ."

In the red-gold light of the fire, Sandy saw something he'd never seen on anyone's face before when looking at him, not even his parents.

Peregrine looked at Sandy like he was everything in the entire world.

No. Sandy refused to melt for that. He was indeed everything to Peregrine, because he was the key to Peregrine's revenge, and that was the only reason.

"Seems a little unproductive to worry when you plan on killing me anyway," Sandy pointed out, annoyed and hopeless and hurt and suddenly so very tired. He wanted to be in a warm bed, in a warm room, with a warm lover petting him until he fell asleep—and damn it all to hell, he wasn't picturing his townhome in London when he thought this, but the priory and his captive's cell within it. And Peregrine Hind cradling him as he drifted into sweet, satisfied dreams.

"Alexander," Peregrine said, his voice frayed.

"Don't *Alexander* me, everyone calls me Sandy anyway, and you're going to *kill* me, and—"

"I'm not going to kill you," the highwayman said softly. "Alexander. You're safe. I'm not going to hurt you."

It took a moment for the words to sink in. Sandy tucked his lower lip between his teeth and then released it. "Explain yourself."

Peregrine, against all odds, gave a short little laugh. "There's nothing to explain," he said, looking down at Sandy. "I won't kill you. I don't think I'm capable of it at this point. Maybe I could have done it in that very first moment, when I knew nothing of you except your relationship to the duke, but then again, maybe not. I haven't killed since the war, and I—"

He sighed. "I can't kill our chickens or pheasants at the priory. I can't even hunt. I don't . . . I don't like it, how it feels. I don't like how the nightmares still come to me sometimes, full of the voices of the dead. So I don't know if I could have done it that night anyhow, but it hardly matters, does it, because now I *do* know you. I know how you smile and how you sigh, and the thought of you being hurt is like a bayonet through the throat."

Sandy's heart tilted and slid against his ribs, a thudding, foolish pulp of an organ. Because it wanted so badly to *hope*, and how asinine was that, that it only took a man saying he wasn't going to kill him to make Sandy all doe-eyed?

"You really don't want to kill me?" Sandy asked. "But what about Reginald? The ransom?"

"I don't know," Peregrine confessed, dropping his face closer to Sandy. "But a couple days ago, you said I might decide to keep you. What if I did?"

Sandy didn't have an answer to that. He knew of lovers in the Second Kingdom who chose to have masters or mistresses in private—to be a captive of sorts to their lover's commands. But it was always chosen in the normal circumstances when it came to sex and love and play.

These were not the normal circumstances.

"You truly won't kill me?" Sandy whispered.

"I won't."

"And you won't allow one of your band to kill me?"

"I won't," Peregrine repeated firmly. "You are safe with me. With us. I'm sorry that I didn't tell you this sooner—that I didn't see it sooner. When I think of being apart from you . . . " Peregrine didn't finish his sentence.

Instead, he brushed his mouth over Sandy's with a kiss that felt as vulnerable as it was brief. The highwayman was still trembling, Sandy realized, still shaking with relief and maybe other emotions too raw to name.

Sandy was shaking too. It felt too good to be true, and he didn't know if it was hope or doubt that made him shiver so.

And then Peregrine's mouth was back on Sandy's again, hungrier this time, the relief tasting so much like urgent, clawing need, and Sandy felt the same need rising in his blood. There was so much he didn't know, so much he didn't trust and so much he hoped for anyway, but this—*this* —he knew. He knew flesh, he knew groans and throbs and seed.

He pressed himself tighter to the highwayman, sliding his hands up to Peregrine's neck as Peregrine kissed him again and again, his hot tongue slashing into Sandy's mouth with desperate strokes, and then they were stumbling back, back until Sandy was against the wall. Below, their hips met and pressed and rubbed, and Peregrine braced his hands on either side of Sandy's head so he could push in harder, grind his hips against Sandy's even more. Their clothed cocks slipped rigid and thick against each other's, and Peregrine's kisses were so, so hot, and Sandy couldn't stand another moment without Peregrine inside him, he simply couldn't.

He struggled out of the coat and then unbuttoned his breeches, turning as he did.

"Alexander," Peregrine groaned, and Sandy decided right then and there that he liked when Peregrine called him that. He hardly ever heard *Alexander*; he'd been *Sandy* since he was a child. The irrelevant spare, the pet. But Peregrine used his full name like he was a king or an emperor.

A ruler in his own right.

It used to scare him, that possibility, whenever he thought of what might happen if he was still Reginald's heir when Reginald died and had to take over the Second Kingdom. It still did terrify him, but for the first time in his life, it electrified him a little too. Like maybe he could be a ruler if Peregrine thought he could be.

"Don't make me wait," Sandy said breathlessly, bracing his hands next to Peregrine's on the wall. "*Please.*"

The highwayman uttered a soft oath, but his hands dropped to his own breeches, and then Alexander heard him spitting into his palm.

"You wanted it like a soldier?" Peregrine asked, the wet, blunt head of his cock entreating entrance to Sandy's body. "This is much the same."

Then a thrust which felt like a sword of fire.

Sandy had done this before—a rake didn't fuck his way through London without the occasional impromptu swive with no oil on hand—so the initial discomfort wasn't a surprise. What was a surprise was the man behind him, who wasn't trying to hammer in and out right away, who added more slickness when it was needed, who was already reaching around to take Sandy's erection in his calloused palm and giving it rough, satisfying pumps as he let Sandy adjust to him.

Maybe it was the hand pleasuring him, or maybe it was the time Peregrine gave Sandy to relax into the invasion—or maybe it was just that it was Peregrine Hind, and with him, Sandy felt a deeply arousing combination of imperiled and safe.

Whatever it was, he was soon panting and moaning into the wall, rocking his prick into Peregrine's hand, fucking himself back on the thief. Which had Peregrine rubbing oh so wonderfully against the essential spot inside him. Sandy's testicles drew up tighter to his body, and astonishingly fast, he felt himself ready to surge in Peregrine's grip.

"Soldiers," Sandy gasped, "can't have been this considerate."

"Consideration is a rare thing in the tents," Peregrine admitted.

"Show me."

"As you wish," Peregrine grunted, drawing back to give

Sandy a series of rough strokes that had his knees threatening to buckle.

The grunting behind him continued, each grunt matched with an arrow of pleasure right through Sandy's core, stabbing up into his belly, and he watched the big shadow on the wall behind him, all male, all brutal, all hellbent on this raw, primal act.

With Peregrine's cock hot and stroking, with the sound of the highwayman's pleased grunts and the crackle of the fire, Sandy's climax tore through him, tore him right in half. He let out a long cry that was nearly a wail, his organ seizing hard in Peregrine's fist and then striping the wall in front of him with seed.

All of him must have been clenching and contracting, even the hole Peregrine was fucking, because Peregrine gave an animal noise and followed Sandy over the edge, his hips working to keep himself deep as he emptied himself into the man he had pinned against the wall.

They both panted there for a moment, breathing hard, slumping forward until Sandy's head was against the roughly plastered wall and Peregrine's was against the back of Sandy's neck.

"What do you think of the soldier's way of doing things?" Peregrine asked, and Sandy just laughed.

"I think I'm ready to enlist tomorrow."

Nine

PEREGRINE

"I'M PLENTY WARM," Alexander fussed as Peregrine tried to layer his coat over the one Alexander was already wearing. "You've built a fire big enough for a Viking hall."

That demonstrably wasn't true, but Peregrine didn't argue, only settled back against the wall. There were chairs here, but he'd chosen the floor because then he could sit with Alexander between his legs and have him recline on his chest while they waited out the storm. It had begun raining outside, a thick, drenching deluge, and the coming of dawn did little to lighten the world. Peregrine was grateful to his past self for having the patience and foresight to keep this place well stocked with things for a fire.

"This isn't a Viking hall," Alexander said after a moment, squirming to get comfortable against Peregrine's chest. "But it's no shepherd's hut either. Clearly, it was a farmhouse."

"There was a whole hamlet here once. You'll see the empty houses in the daylight when we leave."

"An entire hamlet? Empty? Why do you think they left?"

Peregrine had refused to talk about his past for so long that he was surprised to hear the words fall from his lips. "Most of them couldn't make a living here anymore and had to move. But the people in this particular house died."

"Died?" Alexander said, clearly horrified. "Recently?"

"Six years ago now."

"*How?*"

Peregrine looked over at the fireplace, crackling with a fire just as it had in his earliest memories. "The short answer is a fever."

"And the long answer?"

Peregrine watched the flames dance behind the old fire-dogs, thinking of the day he'd gone to enlist, of his mother setting his coat and boots by the fire so they'd be warm when he left. It was strange how such a vast tree of catastrophes could come from a single seed. "The eldest son left them. Their father had been dead a while, and so he was the head of the family for a time. But he knew he would never marry, never sire children, and so he thought it best to leave the farm to his younger brother. He would go off and earn good wages to send home instead. But it's nearly impossible to send letters to infantry when they're at war, and so he didn't know that the Duke of Jarrell had decided to enclose the common land shared by everyone in the hamlet. The land they used for farming, for grazing, for their living, was gone. They'll hang a lowborn man for stealing more than twelve pence, but if a lord steals the income and sustenance from an entire village, he is given an Act of Parliament to do so and then he's heralded as a reformer and a modern man."

Peregrine took a long breath, the injustice of it burning him all over again. He had to make himself go back to the story, back to the house and the family who'd lived in it, other-wise he'd jump to his feet in a seething rage and go find the duke right then and there. "Half-starving, the sister found a way to approach the duke and plead their case. He offered her some small assistance in exchange for time spent in his bed. She agreed, because what other choice did she have?"

Alexander had gone still against his chest. "And then?" he asked quietly.

"And then the fever came," Peregrine told him. "It took the mother and the brother quickly. The sister hung on, but by this point she was swollen with the duke's child, and she never truly recovered. The duke, of course, wasn't interested in a mistress who was pregnant *or* sickly, and so refused to help or even see her. It was beyond foolish to go to Far Hope the night she died, but she must have felt it was the only place she could go. Perhaps she thought if the duke could see her, he would take pity on her for the unborn child's sake? Perhaps she thought a servant would help? No one can say. But whatever she thought, it didn't happen. Even though the night was bitterly cold and she was very ill, no one admitted her into the house. The next morning, they found her with frost on her eyelashes and no breath left in her at all."

Alexander's voice was both sad and careful when he asked, "And the eldest son? The one who went to war?"

Peregrine took his eyes from the fire and occupied himself with Alexander's hair instead, curling the silken ends around his fingers as he spoke. "He came home a year after the sister had died and learned the story from a neighboring vicar. He found his childhood home empty, his childhood village empty, and his family in their new graves. He learned that it was the duke who had enclosed the land, starved his family, coerced his sister into his bed and then left her to die. Everything the son had become a soldier for was gone, and all the blood and death and disease he'd endured because it earned money for his family was for nothing in the end. Nothing at all."

Alexander moved so Peregrine could more easily stroke his hair. "But how did you decide to become a highwayman then?" he asked, pushing past the pretense that the story had been about anyone else. "The revenge—I see that well enough now. But why become *the* Peregrine Hind to achieve it?"

"It was an accident the first time," Peregrine said, remembering a long-ago summer evening. He'd been staying in his vacant family home after learning what had happened, lost to his grief. "There was a riding party, out quite late. Your brother wanted to show his guests the enclosed fields, boast about how much his new flock had already earned for him, and so they were riding down my lane outside."

Peregrine had stood inside his doorway like a ghost, watching as the duke had proudly told this fine, mounted party how much he'd improved the land, how he'd turned the commons from inefficient wastes into wool and then into money. And as Peregrine listened, the fathomless pain which had gnawed at him for days—which had stolen his thoughts, his sensations, even his ability to sleep and to feed himself— had forged itself into a blade, and that blade cut through his grief. That blade gave him purpose.

And that was when Peregrine had known he was going to kill the duke.

"Fine people are so careless," Peregrine continued. "I watched as they milled around the shell of my dead hamlet, paying as much mind to me as they would one of the duke's new sheep. They had servants behind them with a cart in case they'd like to stop and have a drink or something to eat, and the cart was loaded with silver and dishes. The silver alone would have fed the village for a year or more." He paused, thinking of how it had felt to see the Duke of Jarrell call for an alfresco celebration of his successful wool venture, to see the servants open the lid of the chest on the cart and reveal gleaming silver and glass. To watch these people toast the destruction and the hunger and the death that had made the rich duke so much richer still.

It had felt like standing in front of his family's graves all over again.

"I thought, here is my chance to kill the duke," Peregrine said. "He was right there, standing like a lazy pheasant in front of my family's house, ignoring my presence and swilling wine. I'd newly come from the war, and I still had my pistols. I wouldn't even have had to leave the house . . ."

"But you didn't succeed," Alexander surmised.

"I missed. Not by much, but enough to warn him. The entire party fled down the lane in terror, thinking they were all being hunted, and the servants ran on foot after them."

"Leaving the silver," Alexander concluded.

"Leaving the silver," Peregrine said in confirmation. After staring at the booty for several minutes, Peregrine had decided he had no need of it. He'd found the other families who'd fled the hamlet and gave the silver to them in its entirety. "At first, I thought I'd stalk the road to find the duke again, get on with my revenge, and then I would—well, I wasn't sure what I would do after. But it didn't matter at first, because I couldn't find him. Only other dawdling lords and ladies, slowly rolling through the hills with jewels and coins and anything else you could think of. All on their way to Far Hope, for one party or another. It was too easy, and out on the moors, it's even easier not to get caught after, not if you grew up here and know where to hide. Not if you made friends in every town and village by giving away so much of what you've stolen."

"And so you became a fearsome highwayman entirely incidentally."

Peregrine leaned his head back against the wall, watching the rain sluice down the small window's warped panes. "It was the only thing that felt right," he admitted. "I had no farm left, no family, and I couldn't make myself go back to the army. And I liked how it felt, taking from these people who had so much and giving it to the people who had so little. Soon others joined me, Lyd—your relation by marriage, you know —joined me too."

"*Lydia*," Alexander breathed, shaking his head against Peregrine's chest in disbelief. "I hadn't seen her since she was a girl, but I should have known it was her. No wonder she was so excited to rob Judith."

Peregrine made a noise of assent.

"I know it means very little in the face of what you've lost, but I couldn't be sorrier for what Reginald has done to you and those you loved," Alexander said. "And thank you for telling me what happened, even though I'm probably the last person you want to share your past with."

The rain was so loud, so insistent, but it was almost soothing now, like it was washing away everything that wasn't this moment, that wasn't Alexander cuddled sweetly against Peregrine's chest.

"You're the only one I've ever told the entire story to," Peregrine said. "I don't know why I've never told anyone else —I suppose because it hurt so much to think about. It hurt to think that I sailed off and left my family at the mercy of the world. I never even had the chance to apologize for how I failed them. Their graves were already sprouting grass by the time I'd returned."

"Oh, Peregrine," Alexander said softly. "It wasn't your fault. If you'd been here, you wouldn't have been able to stop Reginald either. In fact, you might be dead of that same fever too."

Peregrine had to concede that this was true.

"And," Alexander added, "perhaps it hurts precisely because you haven't told anyone. You've been carrying it alone, when no one should carry something like that inside their own minds and nowhere else."

"That's very wise."

"Well," Alexander murmured, tucking his hands inside

Peregrine's coat, "people have always said that wisdom is my greatest virtue."

"They have not."

"You're right," Alexander said, clearly fighting a yawn. "You've already had my greatest virtue spending all over the wall of your family home."

Peregrine snorted, and together they subsided into a gentle silence, which was all the gentler for the harsh rememberings which had come before it.

Peregrine was used to the past feeling like a broken mirror inside him, like what had happened existed only in shards and splinters in his memory, glinting and ready to cut. But this was the first time he'd ever told the entire story aloud, with all its crimes and abuses, and in the order that they'd happened. It slotted all his memories into their proper places, and now that he'd fitted the pieces of the mirror together, he could finally see what it reflected. Still horror, still pain—but it no longer felt like it was slicing him with every step he took.

He was still angry, yes, but now the anger was inside him, and not the other way around.

After four years, it was like a gift and being unmade at the same time. He felt picked apart at the seams; he felt like an unstitched doll, or the pieces of a coat laid out on a tailor's table. He didn't know what to do with himself. The only thing he did know was that the unstitching was all to do with the man in his arms, the man who'd made him smile and laugh and—and *hope*—after these many years of living in his broken-mirror world.

He held his lover, who'd now drifted all the way off to sleep, tighter and tried not to think about what would happen if Alexander left him. If he couldn't keep this sweet, spoiled rake for his own.

* * *

THE RAIN DIED down a few hours later, and Alexander stirred as Peregrine carefully extracted himself from their embrace and went to ready the horse. The younger man was yawning in the doorway as Peregrine approached with his saddled mount.

"We should go back to the priory," said Peregrine.

Alexander blinked at him. His cheeks were flushed from sleep, his hair tousled, and his eyes pupil-blown from the dim interior of the longhouse. "Am I still your prisoner?" he asked quietly.

"I don't know," Peregrine said, just as quietly. "Will you try to escape again if you are?"

"Yes," replied Alexander. "Will you try to catch me again?"

Peregrine looked at him. "Do you want me to?"

Alexander looked at the ground, his lashes long against his cheeks and his breathing deep as if he were confronting some uncomfortable truth. Finally, he answered. "Yes."

Peregrine's own breath stuttered and then filled his lungs, as if Alexander's answer were the only air he needed to breathe. Whatever was between them wouldn't end now, thank every god and spirit who'd ever been worshipped in these lonely hills.

With heady relief and an even headier greed coursing through his veins, Peregrine held out his hand to take Alexander's, and with hands linked, they began to walk down the lane, Peregrine leading the horse behind them.

$$Ten$$

PEREGRINE

THE TRIP back to the priory didn't feel nearly long enough to Peregrine. He supposed it was because once they returned, they'd have to decide what happened next and whether he would release Alexander for real. Whether he would still attempt to claim a ransom from the duke . . . whether he would build new plans for killing Reginald and fulfilling his revenge.

As they walked through the newly washed world, with its trees and shrubs bleeding into the jewel tones of autumn—and as he held Alexander's hand tighter than was necessary, pulling him close, savoring his rake's eternal Christmas scent—Peregrine wondered if his appetite for revenge had dulled somewhat. If the blade which had once cut through his grief and pain had finally blunted itself. Or had been blunted by the mere existence of Lord Alexander Dartham.

Alexander, who was everything he should hate and somehow, everything he needed instead.

They arrived at the priory, and as they entered the stables, they saw the horses belonging to the other thieves already munching hay inside their stalls. They took care of the animal and then went inside the church, where the gang was gathered with a hearty meal and a few open bottles of wine. They were clearly a few cups in, most of them sitting with their boots propped on the table and roaring with laughter at each other's stories.

"I take it the robbery went well?" Peregrine asked Lyd as they approached the table.

"There was no robbery," Lyd said. "And where *were* you two?"

"I tried to escape," Alexander volunteered. "It was a very good escape, if you must know."

"Why was there no robbery?" Peregrine asked, ignoring Alexander. "Did the duchess take another road to Far Hope?"

"And why didn't you just tell me you were Judith's cousin!" Alexander burst out. "I would have begged you to help me escape!"

Lyd had made grown men piss themselves for taking such a tone with her, so Peregrine was genuinely shocked when she answered, almost kindly, "Because I didn't trust you to be any different than your brother or sister-in-law, Lord Alexander, and I wasn't interested in helping a Dartham with anything. But things have changed."

"They have?" Alexander asked, confused.

Lyd gave them both a look and sighed. "I think you deserve some privacy for this. Follow me."

They went into the sacristy. Lyd didn't bother closing the door, but her voice was quiet as she told them, "The duchess is dead."

Next to him, Alexander went still in a way that Peregrine had learned meant he was upset. Without thinking about it,

Peregrine drew him close, wrapping an arm around his lover's slender waist.

Lyd's eyebrow raised at the familiar gesture, but she didn't remark on it. Their crowd was rather free with lovers, men and women alike, although it had to be said that Peregrine would be the first in their group to consort with someone he'd halted on the road.

"How did she die?" Alexander asked, his voice small.

"Whatever illness she had was worse than anyone thought, at least according to the innkeeper. She died there at the inn, and her body is being taken to Far Hope now."

Lyd's voice was level, factual, but her shoulders were loose and her eyes clear. Peregrine met her gaze, and she gave him a short nod. They had years of silent communication between them, and he knew what she was saying. She would never have her moment of justice with Judith, but the relief of Judith never being able to hurt her again was enough.

"Her husband is ill now too," Lyd added. "The same malady, most likely."

Fear flashed through Peregrine, hot and bright. If Reginald was also sick, and they'd all been traveling together . . .

"Alexander, you haven't been—you're not feeling ill?"

"We didn't see each other before we set out, and then we took separate coaches after Basingstoke so she could be more comfortable," Alexander replied faintly "I don't feel sick in the least."

The relief that flooded through Peregrine then nearly knocked him over. If Alexander took ill—if Alexander *died*— no. He couldn't bear it. The very thought made Peregrine feel like he was being drawn and quartered.

Lyd had paused, as if considering how to phrase what she was going to say next. "His doctor is saying he might only have a few days left."

Alexander was like a statue in Peregrine's hold, unmoving, maybe unbreathing, and Peregrine pulled him closer, wrapped him in both arms. And instead of burrowing into him, instead of pouting or whining or rattling off a hundred different thoughts, Alexander was completely still. When Peregrine moved back and lifted Alexander's face to his, his chest hurt at the sight.

He'd seen more life in a child's doll than in Alexander's face right now.

Peregrine should have welcomed the news about the duke with pleasure, exultation even, but now he felt . . . nothing. No pleasure, no relief.

His enemy was dying, and the only thing he felt was worry for Alexander. All he wanted to do was make everything better, *fix* this or ease this for him somehow. His sweet rake hadn't wanted to be the duke or the leader of the Second Kingdom, and now the possibility was bearing down on him like a runaway coach—it would run him over whether he was ready or not.

And that Alexander's worst fear would come on the heels of his brother's death . . .

Peregrine felt something shift inside him, as if some final, vital seam had been ripped open. As if the Peregrine Hind of four hours ago really had been nothing more than those unstitched pieces on a table.

He would have to be made into something new. And whatever it would be, he wanted that something to put Alexander first, always.

"I'll take you to him," Peregrine said.

"What?" Alexander asked.

"*What?*" demanded Lyd.

Peregrine turned so he could see Alexander's face, cupping his jaw so he could look into Alexander's dark eyes. Even though there was a table of carousing thieves in the next room over, even though Lyd was watching them with a curious, perceptive stare, it almost felt like they were alone. "I didn't get to say goodbye to my mother or my siblings before they died, and I don't want that for you. You should be with him. You should be home."

"But you hate Reginald," Alexander whispered.

"I do. But what I feel for you," Peregrine whispered back, pressing his forehead against Alexander's, "is stronger than any hatred. It's fiercer than any revenge."

"Oh," Alexander said, his breath catching a little. "Oh."

"Yes," Peregrine said, affirming the unspoken questions in those *ohs*. Whatever the questions were, Peregrine knew the answer was *yes*.

"But I never wanted to see him before now," Alexander said after a moment. "What if he doesn't deserve a goodbye?"

"I know with certainty that he doesn't," replied Peregrine. "But you do."

Alexander met the highwayman's gaze with raw blue eyes. "I thought you'd be happier about this. About him dying."

"I would have been," Peregrine admitted. "Up until this very week. But telling you about what happened has made it easier to bear. And not only speaking of it, but speaking of it to you. You are so much to me, so much more than . . . " He trailed off, uncertain of how to frame what he meant. Alexander had shown him the way to something other than grief and anger; Alexander was a future filled with hope and possibility when before there'd only been an agony-laden past.

"I thought his death would kill my grief," Peregrine started again, still trying to explain. "I thought his suffering would ease my own. But suffering cannot be bought or sold like that, and neither can grief. I am so—"

Here he stopped, aware of Lyd watching them, of the

other thieves nearby. Aware that the words he was about to utter were in no way adequate in the face of what he'd done.

"I'm so ashamed, Alexander. I was so ready to spill Dartham blood that it stopped mattering who carried it in their veins. I'm ashamed that I scared you, threatened you, and made you bargain for your life. And I'm ashamed that I ever once entertained the idea of killing you."

Peregrine took Alexander's hand and laced his fingers through his, bringing the younger man's knuckles to his mouth to kiss. "But more than being ashamed, I am sorry. Sorry past what my words can describe. I won't ask forgiveness for it. But I want you to know that you're safe from me."

"I think," Alexander said, his eyes searching Peregrine's face, "I must have known that, deep down. I think I knew I was safe from the beginning. After all," he said, the corner of his mouth lifting, "not many captors take the trouble to find silk for their captive's wrists instead of rope."

Peregrine smiled back. "If I'd known how much you would enjoy the silk, I would have bound your entire body in it."

Despite everything, Alexander's pupils dilated with interest. "There will be time," he murmured.

Peregrine didn't think so, but he didn't say that out loud. Getting Alexander to Far Hope was the main thing, and if he cast any doubt on their being together in the future, Alexander might react like . . . well, like Alexander.

Perhaps not. Perhaps Alexander would understand. Perhaps he'd even be relieved that Peregrine saw the future so sensibly. But speed was of the essence, and Peregrine couldn't risk this conversation now. It would have to happen later, if it ever did.

"I'll ready a fresh horse," Peregrine said. "Gather what you need and then meet me outside."

* * *

THE SUN WAS SINKING as they rode, but at least the wind was mild and the skies newly free of clouds. Alexander chattered the entire way about how much the Second Kingdom would love Peregrine, even though he'd openly robbed a fair number of them by now, and about where Peregrine could sleep, and about how Alexander would make sure Peregrine didn't have to see the duke while he was at Far Hope.

Peregrine recognized the chatter as Alexander's way of deflecting worry about his brother—and likely also the possibility of becoming the duke—and let him continue. It seemed to make him feel better, and if he had the notion that Peregrine would be staying with him at Far Hope, then Peregrine still didn't have the heart to disabuse him of it. Especially after hearing Alexander's nervous prattle, after observing his rigid but trembling form as they rode.

Alexander would find out soon enough when they got there, and in the future, he would thank Peregrine for his level-headedness. After all, it was absurdity to think that the duke could openly parade a male lover around London, and even more absurdity when the lover in question was a notorious criminal.

And even if the Second Kingdom wouldn't mind, Alexander would be a duke. He'd have a responsibility to marry and sire heirs, and Peregrine didn't think he could survive watching Alexander marry someone else. He didn't want to be a mistress, tucked away somewhere, contributing to yet another unhappy aristocratic marriage. It sounded like a way for three people to be miserable—but if he left, he could lower that number to one.

Himself.

Highwaymen didn't get happy endings. They didn't die

old and gray in a lover's arms. They died young and they died alone.

But it was no use trying to explain this to Alexander. He wouldn't accept that some things were out of even a rake's reach.

Or a duke's.

It was fully dark by the time they reached the narrow vale of the Hope Valley and passed through the crooked standing stones at its entrance. A shallow river wound beside the road as they rode through the small village, and then, after a mile or so, the stern edifice of Far Hope revealed itself, its many windows glowing against the dark.

Somehow, that didn't make it seem any more welcoming to Peregrine. It rather reminded him of lights along a rampart or behind a defensive ditch, like Far Hope was a fortress enduring on from a grimmer time. Hardly where he would have expected a hidden society of hedonism and pleasure—but then again, perhaps that was why the Second Kingdom was there. Far Hope did feel like a castle of its own remote kingdom, set in a land even emperors and kings had struggled to properly conquer.

"It used to be an abbey," Alexander said, talking in that quick, overly bright way. "A Saxon one, and then a Norman one, which was converted and partially swallowed up by the medieval manor house. That's why it's so irregular—they say the tower there was originally a bell tower for the abbey church, but that may just be a story. I'll take you up there, though, so you can see the views in daylight, because it's fantastic, a vista like nothing else."

Peregrine made noises of acknowledgment as they rode through the open gate to the house. He came to a stop in front of the large wooden door at the front and then he held the reins for Alexander's horse as Alexander dismounted.

His former captive looked up at him. With the light

coming from the manor house, half his face was cast in gold and the other in pure shadow.

"You're not getting off with me?" Alexander asked. "Oh," he went on, still with that brittle, fast tone, "of course, you're going to go to the stables first. I can come with you if you'd like. Or wait here, and then we can go in together."

"Go see your brother," Peregrine said, as gently as a man like him was capable. "He'll be grateful to see you alive and well and free."

Alexander made a face. "If that's true, it'll only be because he will savor not paying a ransom, even on his deathbed."

"Perhaps. But there's only one way to know."

Alexander hesitated. "You are coming too, right? You don't have to see him, but you can stay here, and . . . " He stopped. Maybe he was realizing, as Peregrine already had, that in sickness, death, funeral arrangements, and becoming a peer, there wouldn't be much room for a kept lover. Especially one that was officially wanted for crimes punishable by death.

"I think we both know the answer to that, Alexander," Peregrine said.

In the gold-hued light, Peregrine could see the quiver in Alexander's beautiful mouth.

He knew exactly how Alexander felt right now because Peregrine felt the same. Like his heart was being torn out.

"Stay well," Peregrine said quietly. "You aren't allowed to take ill, do you understand? Say your goodbyes at a distance and listen to everything the physician tells you."

"If I take ill, will you come here right away?" the rake said, mouth continuing to tremble, but with petulance now as well as hurt.

Peregrine gave him his sternest look. "*Alexander.*"

Alexander swallowed, stepping back in time for Peregrine to see a tear glittering its way down his high-boned cheek. It took everything Peregrine had not to haul the rake back in his arms where he belonged, but somehow, he managed. Somehow, he kept his tears to himself. Even though he'd just surrendered everything he'd held on to for the last four years.

He'd given up revenge. He'd given up Alexander.

What did he have left now?

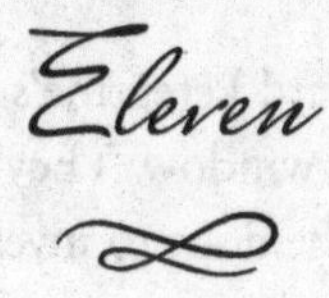

Eleven

SANDY

"**WILL** you not at least kiss me goodbye then?" Sandy asked, his voice thick and his eyes burning. He was panicked and he was numb; he was furious and he was frozen with hurt.

He was everything and nothing all at once, and it was this horrible highwayman's fault.

"You will cheat and pull me off my horse if I lean down to kiss you," said Peregrine with a fond smile.

"Of course I will," Sandy managed to huff. His throat ached so much he couldn't stand it. "You can't mean to leave me here, can you? You can't mean to ride off in the dark and not stay?"

"Think of it as your escape," Peregrine told him. His voice was gentle. "You've escaped me now. You're free."

"Goddammit, Peregrine, you cannot just *leave* me like this!" Sandy said furiously, another tear tracking down his cheek. He realized, distantly, that it was the first time he'd cried all week. Even being kidnapped, threatened with death, and used as a pawn against his brother hadn't made him cry. But this—Peregrine just *leaving* him here when he needed him most—

When Peregrine didn't answer, Sandy asked desperately, "But I will see you again, right? Soon? When everything is settled?"

He took a step toward Peregrine's horse right as a shadow passed behind a nearby window. They'd been heard, and soon someone would be at the door to investigate. Peregrine sighed as Sandy reached out to put a hand on the highwayman's thigh. It was firm and unyielding, like the man it belonged to. Sandy wished he had the strength to drag Peregrine from his horse. He wished he were strong enough to abduct Peregrine as Peregrine had abducted him.

It couldn't be that he'd spent years chasing the hope of something solid and real, only to find it and then lose it within a matter of days. It made no sense, practically or cosmically. Sandy was Lord Alexander Dartham, and he could do almost anything he wanted. And if the worst happened and he was made the duke, the *only* consolation to such a horror would be the power to have the lover he wanted in his bed.

No, he wouldn't stand for this. He couldn't. If he didn't have this highwayman with him, then he wouldn't survive whatever came next, and he wouldn't want to, and—

Peregrine's hand came over his. It was cold, since he'd ridden without gloves, but it was so big and so strong. It completely covered Sandy's hand and pinned it hard to the warm thigh underneath.

"Yes, Alexander." Peregrine's voice was low and rough, but steady as stone. "You'll see me again once everything is settled."

Sandy looked up into the thief's eyes, which glittered with the light from Far Hope. "You swear?" Sandy whispered.

Peregrine gave Sandy's hand a hard, long squeeze. "I swear. Now go, fast. Your brother needs you."

Sandy drank him in with one last glance and then left with an abrupt motion, tearing himself away with all the willpower he had. He had to go to his brother; he had to face whatever fate awaited him.

All he could do was hope that this was not the last he'd seen of Peregrine Hind.

Twelve

SANDY

SIX MONTHS LATER

ALEXANDER DARTHAM, the new Duke of Jarrell, was absolutely fucking miserable.

As if it wasn't bad enough on its own to learn how to run the ducal estate with all its dealings and enterprises, Sandy also had to confront the sheer scale of Reginald's sins. Peregrine's hamlet hadn't been the only village gutted by Reginald's enclosures, and searching for the villagers and cottagers who'd migrated away so Sandy could offer some kind of restitution was long, difficult work. Some had gone to towns where they had relations; some had tried to eke out a new living elsewhere in the countryside. Some had gone all the way to London, and one family had even emigrated to America. But with the help of the Foscourts, he managed to find a way. Sandy liked to think that he would have tried to ameliorate the wounds Reginald had left behind even if he'd never met Peregrine Hind, but he couldn't deny that it was Peregrine's face he saw in his thoughts when he directed his lawyers to issue payments, Peregrine's voice he heard in his mind when he read the letters of thanks some of villagers sent in return.

And while Sandy didn't miss Reginald and Judith in the usual ways of grief, he had to accept that their deaths still affected him—perhaps more so for the complicated relationships he'd had with them before they died. Figuring out how to mourn while figuring out how to duke was already unpleasant. Added to his new responsibilities with the Second Kingdom and the continual ache in his chest from Peregrine's absence, it was torment.

And after months had passed and his highwayman still hadn't returned, Sandy didn't even bother trying the things that he used to do in order numb his unhappiness. There was no amount of bed-play or gambling or wine that would erase the truth.

Peregrine Hind, the first person Sandy had ever fallen in love with, had lied. He wasn't coming back.

Sandy was alone, and there was a beautiful irony to that.

He had placed his bloody, trusting heart in Peregrine's hands the night the highwayman had ridden away from him, having no idea that the thief would trample it underneath his steed's hooves the minute he turned and left. Sandy had hoped and longed and *cared* like he never had before, and it was thrown back in his face every day that Peregrine didn't come back.

He was haunted and bereft, and so, in a perverse way, Peregrine had his revenge against the Dartham family at long last.

Because the Duke of Jarrell was as miserable as a living person could be.

* * *

ONE OF THE first things he'd done as the duke was return Lyd's family property to her, which had been a fucking *headache*, since thieves were not generally reachable by mail or courier. He'd had to personally loiter on the road to Exeter for several nights in a row, having his driver roll an unmarked but expensive carriage back and forth for hours until he'd finally baited Lyd out of hiding. The first thing he'd done when he'd been hauled out of his carriage by Ned was to search for Peregrine's grim face and broad shoulders. When he couldn't find his highwayman among the band, his shoulders had slumped and his heart had slowly slid into his stomach, where it sat there like a dead, disappointed weight.

"Here," Sandy had said, handing Lyd a sheaf of paper when she'd grumpily lowered her pistol after realizing who she was aiming it at. "The property is yours again. Free and clear. Along with the ransom my brother would have paid you."

She'd stared at him, not taking the papers. "Why?"

Sandy had flapped the papers at her. "Because it should have been yours to begin with. And I'm trying to be better than Reginald. And—and—" He made a face, screwing up the courage to say what he needed to say. "And because I'm sorry that I didn't do more to help you when I could have. I could have searched for you after I found out what happened, or tried to get your family land back to you earlier, or at least made better sure that Reginald and Judith would stop searching for you. And I didn't. I'm sorry."

He looked up to see Lyd's mouth twisting to the side—but in thought, not in disgust.

Finally, with a short nod, she took the papers from him. "Very well, then."

"All the rights to the water and the mill have been restored to you," Sandy said. "With that and your share of the ransom, you could live very comfortably without taking to the road ever again."

"Hmm."

Sandy asked, with all the casual charm he could muster, "So, are you still going to rob people?"

Lyd cocked a grin, tossing a look over her shoulder to the other thieves, who were grinning back at her like Sandy had just told an incredible joke. "Maybe," she said with mock-coyness.

"Will you at least stop robbing my guests?"

"Is that a condition of this?" Lyd asked, holding up the papers.

"No," Sandy said honestly. "But it never hurts to ask." He gave her his biggest smile, the one that usually got him whatever he wanted.

She didn't look impressed, but she did say, "I'll think on it."

"You really still prefer this life?" Sandy asked, gesturing to the cold night around them. "Waiting in the cold and in the dark? Robbing people? Fleeing from them?"

Lyd had grinned again. "People flee from *me*, Sandy. Should I go back to embroidery by the window? Sitting quietly in church and thinking of what repairs the dairy will need next year? After I've gone wherever I've liked, done whatever I've liked, and chosen who shares my bed and when? Do you really think I would want to go back to a quiet gentry life after that?"

"Well, when you put it that way," Sandy said. "But there's always the Second Kingdom. I could invite you, you know."

Her smile turned into a baring of teeth. "I don't want your kingdom of rich hypocrites, Sandy."

"I'm trying to make the Kingdom better," Sandy said, a little wearily.

"Is it working?"

Sandy could only be honest. "I don't know," he'd said. "But I have to try, don't I?"

Who else would, if he didn't? He was the duke, and the Kingdom was his. It was his duty to end the petty infighting and favoritism that Reginald had fostered, and he hoped that things were already changing. He only wished he didn't have to do it alone. He had Juliana and her family as staunch allies, and a few other friends in the Kingdom, but he wanted someone at his side, nearby always, holding him at night while he worked through the never-ending list of problems that came with the Kingdom.

He wanted Peregrine.

He finally asked Lyd what he'd been dying to from the moment they'd stopped his carriage. "Is Peregrine with you?"

Lyd gave Sandy a pitying look.

"Please," Sandy said quietly, not above begging, not above demanding they take him captive again just so they could bring him back to Peregrine. "Please, Lydia."

"He isn't with us, Sandy," Lyd said. "I'm sorry."

"No—" he started as she moved back toward the others and their horses. "Lyd, wait—"

But it was too late. They were on their horses and riding away, leaving Sandy only with his driver in the dark. He'd climbed numbly back in the carriage, signaled for the return to Far Hope, and tried not to cry the entire way back. He'd believed Lyd when she said that Peregrine wasn't with them, but then where was he?

Had he retired? Rusticated? Left the country altogether?

God. Was that really so preferable to a life with Sandy?

* * *

"SO YOU'RE NOT PLANNING on marrying? At all?"

Sandy and Juliana Durrington née Foscourt, the daughter of the Earl of Kellow and Sandy's lifelong friend, were walking through the ballroom with stars on the ceiling after a heavy lunch. She'd come to stay for the latest Second Kingdom revel —only the third that Sandy had presided over in the last half year—and he'd shamelessly made her plan the entire thing. It was enough to adjudicate the membership disputes and manage the tangle of internecine politics Reginald had left behind. He couldn't be bothered to plan the menus for the orgies too.

Luckily for him, Juliana lived for such things, and even luckier for him, she was more than happy to seed little rumors on his behalf here and there. Mainly that his current abstention from the pleasures of the Kingdom was due to the loss of his beloved brother and sister-in-law, and for no other more scandalous reason.

Like that he was pining for a lover who didn't want him back—and who was also currently wanted by the Crown.

It was raining buckets and buckets outside, making a dull roar everywhere in the manor house, a roar which echoed the noise inside Sandy's head these days.

He took a minute to answer Juliana's question. "I have a passel of first cousins already, and all of them are breeding like rabbits. There are plenty of heirs with the Dartham name."

Juliana looked over at him. "Are you sure, though?" she asked softly. "A marriage doesn't have to be about heirs alone. A wife could help shoulder the burden of the dukedom and the Second Kingdom. She could make life easier for you—and be a friend and companion."

Sandy cut her a look. "Are you volunteering, Juliana?"

She let out a laugh. "No, no, I'm quite enjoying my new life as a widow. But it's something to consider. You've bedded women before, after all, and you might also find someone who is happy to seek their pleasure outside your bed, if you'd rather not have a sexual relationship."

"I've bedded *everyone* before," Sandy said impatiently.

"But that doesn't mean I'm willing to marry someone so I can have help answering letters."

Juliana seemed to think about that, the silk of her mantua hissing on the ballroom floor and mingling with the sound of the rain as they walked. "It's about him, isn't it?" she asked. "The highwayman?"

Sandy had told Juliana everything once the dust had settled after Reginald and Judith's deaths, and so she knew exactly how much it had gutted Sandy when Peregrine had ridden off into the night.

How much more it had gutted him when Peregrine never came back.

"I'm a goddamn fool," Sandy said bitterly. "I'm here with a broken heart, pathetic and moping, and he's probably off kidnapping some other future duke and tying him to a bed."

"Didn't you tell me that he'd been living like a monk before you?" Juliana asked. "And at any rate, he's not kidnapping anyone, *or* even robbing travelers anymore. He's disappeared."

"He's *what*?" asked Sandy.

"I'm shocked you haven't heard. I thought you'd searched for him?"

"I went to the priory two months or so after Reginald died, but it had been abandoned. I'd thought they must have moved their hideout because of me . . . I hadn't realized they'd stopped altogether."

Maybe Lyd had listened to his advice after he'd given her the rights to her property back. Maybe she'd settled down with her house and her money and taken up a nice, quiet hobby that didn't involve pistols.

"*Peregrine Hind* hasn't been seen on the road," Juliana said. "But his former band has. Led by a woman, they say."

Ah. Well, that was Lyd for you.

"Sandy," Juliana said in the careful voice of a friend about to point out the obvious. "Have you given any thought as to why he'd stay away?"

"Of course I have," snapped Sandy. "Because I'm a Dartham, and I'm everything he hates and because I complained too much about the wine when I was his captive."

Juliana stopped walking, turning to face Sandy with a look that was both impatient and pitying. "No, you fopdoodle. He's staying away because he thinks there's no place in your life for him."

Sandy nearly sputtered. "That's ridiculous. I told him all about the Second Kingdom. He should know that in our world—"

Juliana waved a hand. "You don't live your entire life in the Second Kingdom, Sandy. He would know that you'd be expected to marry and that you'd have duties in London to fulfill. And he would know even inside the Second Kingdom that there'd be plenty of people whom he'd robbed and who wouldn't exactly be happy to see him at your right hand. If I were him, I would assume that staying in your life would not only compromise you as the duke, but as the leader of Second Kingdom as well, and that he could love you best by giving you the very thing you wanted most when you were his captive: freedom from him."

Alexander frowned. "But then why not just *say* all that to me? I could have told him immediately how wrong he was!"

"Is he wrong?" Juliana asked quietly. "Would it not make your life harder and his less safe to have him at your side?"

Alexander hated that she was right, but he couldn't deny it. "A wanted criminal does have some inconveniences as a lover," he finally admitted. "But I—"

He stopped, clarity coming like the rain outside, cold and drenching.

"I am a duke now," he said, realizing slowly. "I could fix this."

"You could," Juliana agreed.

"A pardon," said Alexander, getting excited. "James Clavell was issued one, wasn't he? And so many others too! If Peregrine's issued a pardon, then even if a disgruntled member of the Second Kingdom wanted to turn him in, it wouldn't matter."

He paced once and then stopped. "But if I do this, how will I find him to tell him?"

Juliana shrugged. "Think like a highwayman. Where would a highwayman go to hide?"

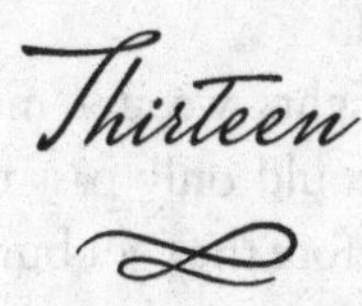

PEREGRINE

A FULL MOON hung over the moors as Peregrine walked along the road. He'd gone up to Lyd's new hideout near her old family home to see how the band was getting on, but they'd been out riding, it seemed, because their new lair was empty. Strange, because it had been Lyd herself to invite him to visit, but Peregrine was made of time now, so what was one wasted day? It wasn't as if he had anything to occupy him other than scratching out a garden in the tiny plots that had been left adjacent to the houses in his village when the fields had been enclosed. It hadn't been enough for the hamlet or even for a family, but for a single person who had the money to buy his own grain rather than grow it, it was serviceable.

He couldn't live like this forever, he knew. Rattling around like a ghost in his childhood home, eating beets and drinking wine while he brooded at the fire. But he also didn't know what else to do. His career as a thief had been so bundled up in the idea of revenge that once he let the revenge go, the idea of stealing no longer held much appeal. He had more than enough to live on, and he'd given so much away to those who needed it most that it no longer felt necessary or interesting to punish the fine people in their fine coaches.

Maybe he was tired.

Or maybe some fights weren't meant to be fought for entire lifetimes. One could only pass their fingers through a flame so many times before they got burned.

Truthfully, though, he knew why he stayed. Why he brooded alone with ghosts instead of finding a new place to live or seeking out some other occupation. The idea of leaving Far Hope's demesne hurt more than he could describe. At least here, he could walk to Alexander's house and watch it from the hills surrounding the valley. At least here, he could sometimes go to the now-empty priory and wander through its abandoned spaces, remembering how it felt that week to have Alexander as his very own.

Peregrine was thinking about all this as he walked through a little valley choked with trees, and that's when he heard a suspicious rustling.

And then a *shh*, and then a horse sprang out in front of him.

"Stand and deliver!" a voice cried out, loud enough to send an owl flapping away in irritation. Peregrine's heart stopped and then skidded back into action with several fast, hungry beats. But not from fear.

He knew that voice. He knew that voice from every dream he'd dreamed in the last six months.

And then the voice said, "Did I say that right? Is that how it goes?"

Lyd—of all fucking people—and Ned and the others stepped out of the shadows to the mounted figure.

"You could have been louder," Lyd said dryly, and then turned to him. "Hello, Peregrine. This is a robbery."

"I thought it was an abduction," said Ned, and Lyd put her palm to her forehead.

"That's right," she said, "this is an abduction. You're being abducted right now."

Peregrine was ignoring them, already walking up to the horse where the mounted rider sat. The rider's hair tumbled over his shoulder in gleaming waves, and his full lips were curled into a secretive little smile.

Just looking at him made Peregrine's chest ache with longing.

"Are you my kidnapper?" asked Peregrine, his heart tumbling all over itself inside his chest, like a newborn foal that couldn't find its legs. He'd tried to stay away from Alexander, tried to do the right thing after so many years of doing the wrong thing, but he couldn't deny that he'd hoped—yearned —for something like this. A moment when he could see Alexander's sparkling eyes again.

"I am your kidnapper," agreed Alexander with great dignity. "I'm here to whisk you away."

Peregrine was very close to Alexander now. He put a possessive hand on the man's thigh, squeezing gently. The feeling of Alexander's warm, lithe muscles under his grip made blood surge to his cock.

"How did you find me?" Peregrine asked.

"Unfortunately, Sandy and I are friends now," Lyd said with a heavy sigh. "And then this week, he popped around my hideout with some sad story about missing you and wanting to see you again."

Peregrine looked to Alexander. "You missed me."

"Yes, you awful, criminal fool, I missed you," replied Alexander impatiently. "I missed you so much that I got a pardon for you from the Crown so that you can come live with me without worrying that someone will inform the local magistrate about a highwayman in my bed."

Peregrine's heart thudded. "You did?"

"I did." Alexander's gaze softened. "You will be safe with me, Peregrine. I swear it."

Peregrine forced himself to think rationally, to think unselfishly. He'd had plenty of time to mull over his decisions, after all, and as much as they hurt—and they really fucking hurt—he still couldn't see that he'd chosen wrongly.

"You'll need to marry," he said softly, his hand lingering possessively on Alexander's thigh. "Have children. I know some married couples are willing to—"

"Ugh, *stop*," Alexander huffed. "I'm not getting married."

"But the dukedom—"

"There are plenty of little ones in line, don't worry about the dukedom and heirs," Alexander said. He reached out to touch Peregrine's jaw with leather-gloved fingertips. "Can't you see, Peregrine Hind?" he whispered. "I only want you. Let me kidnap you, and I swear that I'll make the rest of your life worth it."

"The rest of my life?" Peregrine asked. There was a buzz in his lips, on his tongue, inside his veins.

It felt like hope.

"That's what people do with the ones they love, right?" asked Alexander. "They grow old with them?"

The ones they love.

Yes, somehow, despite everything, those words felt right. As right as a strong horse underneath him, as right as a bright moon on a clear night. As good having a rake tied to his bed.

"If that's the case," Peregrine said, the hope swallowing what was left of his doubts and worries, "then you must know that I want to grow old with you too."

Alexander gave him a big grin—one of those spoiled but bewitching ones Peregrine loved so much—and gestured to an empty cart waiting farther down the road. "Then you must allow to me to get on with my abduction," he said, and Peregrine smiled.

He looked to Lyd, who gave him a mock-salute back. "Thank you for assisting in my kidnapping," he told her as Alexander dismounted with an easy grace and took Peregrine's hand.

"Wouldn't have missed it for all the gold in the kingdom," she said, and then, with a whistle, she and the band moved back toward the trees, where they'd presumably tethered their horses. They waved goodbye, and Peregrine and his captor went to the cart, hitched the horse to the front, and climbed inside.

Alexander at first sat so that he and Peregrine were side by side, but Peregrine had no patience for this, instead pulling Alexander onto his lap and wrapping his arms firmly around Alexander's waist.

Giving a quiet cluck, Alexander took the reins and urged the horse forward to start off for Far Hope.

"I'm nervous your friends in the Second Kingdom won't like me," Peregrine said, his hands beginning to wander all over Alexander's body. It had been so long, so painfully long, and Peregrine's body responded ferociously to the supple duke pressed against him. He also couldn't drag in enough of Alexander's spicy, citrus scent, burying his face in Alexander's hair and breathing it in over and over again.

"You are pardoned now, and you are mine, so they can fuck right off," Alexander said pleasantly. "Besides, they'll eventually see it as a grand story. Anything rare or unusual is like a shiny object to them, I promise you."

"Mm," Peregrine said. He was relieved to hear it, although he knew it might take time for Alexander's world to accept him. Luckily, time was something he was not short on.

"And what role will I be expected to play in this kingdom?" Peregrine asked, still nosing all that soft, wonderful hair. "I have to warn you that I don't want to be with anyone else."

"There's no rule in the kingdom about having to fuck every person you meet." Alexander laughed. "You can be as devoted to me as you like."

"And you?" Peregrine asked, suddenly confronted with the reality that he might have to share his rake. "Will you be . . . partaking in your kingdom?"

Alexander turned, seeming amused. "Why, Peregrine, is that possessiveness I hear in your voice?"

Peregrine growled. Yes, dammit, he was possessive. But he would also give Alexander the world and everything in it, and if Alexander wanted to share his body with people other than Peregrine, then Peregrine would endure—so long it was him Alexander came back to at the end of the night.

Alexander gave Peregrine a soft kiss, then turned and settled against Peregrine's chest. "No," the rake said after a minute, "I don't think I'll be partaking anymore. I may change my mind, of course, I'm flighty like that, but right now all I want is this grim thief I've fallen in love with."

"Truly?"

"I've had the affairs and the games and the pleasures, Peregrine; I've drank fully from every cup I ever found, either at the Kingdom or at court. I want something different now. You."

"I don't want to make you a captive again," Peregrine said. "Please know that. So if you change your mind . . ."

"You'll be the first to know," Alexander promised. "In the meantime, I plan on quenching my insatiate lusts with a certain former solider."

Peregrine growled again, this time in satisfaction, pulling Alexander closer and dropping his hands to Alexander's lap.

"Now, about your captivity," Alexander said, giving a long shudder as Peregrine's fingers began picking open the buttons of his breeches, brushing over the swell of Alexander's erection as they did. "I have some rather—oh, that feels good—"

Peregrine had found Alexander's prick and drawn it out of his clothes, and while the cart pulled them up the road, Peregrine slowly shuttled his grip up and down the stiff flesh. "You were saying?" he murmured into the duke's ear.

"I was saying that I have some rather unusual requests," Alexander said breathlessly, wriggling on Peregrine's lap as Peregrine stroked Alexander's rigidity. It was hot velvet against his palm.

"And what are those?"

"Well, I may b-be the captor this time, but I think you should tie me up. A lot."

Peregrine laughed a little. "I think we can manage that. Anything else?"

"Yes. I know you're no longer filling your nights with crimes on the road. But I won't mind in the least if you're fill your nights being a criminal with *me*."

"And what does a criminal do with you?" Peregrine murmured, loving the feel of Alexander shivering against his chest, the way he rocked against Peregrine's ferocious cockstand.

"Well, I mentioned the tying up," Alexander said, gasping a little. "You could tease me mercilessly. You could deny me until I'm begging for it. You could use me like you did in the farmhouse."

Peregrine's cock jerked against the duke, ready to get started on all those things, but it was his heart which swelled and throbbed the most as he buried his face in Alexander's neck again and inhaled the Christmas scent of his rake-turned-duke-turned-captor. He didn't deserve this—not after the war, not after stalking the roads and raining hellfire upon the travelers he'd found. Not after what he did to Sandy when they first met. But perhaps he could earn it. Earn it like he'd earned peace from his grief over the last six months, earn it like he'd earned the tender, emerald shoots in his new garden behind his family farmhouse. With care and love.

And he knew exactly who he'd care for first.

"In that case, Your Grace," Peregrine said, coaxing Alexander to into a jerking, quivering spend all over his fist, "I shall save all my crimes for you."

"Truly?"

"Every last one."

"Thank God."

And with kisses to his duke's neck, Peregrine took the reins and guided them over the purple moors to Far Hope, and to home.

The end.

***

Want more dangerously sexy stories about Far Hope?

Check out The Conquering of Tate the Pious—a sizzling medieval F/F romance...

England is burning with Norman fires, and Tate—the youngest ever abbess of Far Hope Abbey—is determined to guard the abbey's ancient secrets with her very life. Her life may be what it takes, however, for a Norman warlord known only as The Wolf is pillaging his way right to the abbey's doors. But when The Wolf arrives, Tate finds not the brutal warrior she was expecting, but a cruel and beautiful woman who leads her dead husband's men with a ferocity to rival that of her Viking ancestors. And after she sets eyes on Tate, it becomes clear that gold and silver aren't the only things The Wolf wants to carry off into the night...

Your medieval morality chain romance is waiting!

Also by Sierra Simone

Co-Written with Julie Murphy:

A Merry Little Meet Cute

Snow Place Like LA: A Christmas in July Novella

A Holly Jolly Ever After

The Lyonesse Trilogy:

Salt in the Wound (a free Lyonesse prequel!)

Salt Kiss

Honey Cut

Lyonesse #3

Standalones:

Red & White: an FFM winter story — FREE!

Supplicant: an age gap novella

Sanguine: an MM vampire story

Sherwood: an FFM novella

My Present This Year: a forbidden Christmas story - FREE!

The Priest Series:

Priest

Midnight Mass: A Priest Novella

Sinner

Saint

Thornchapel:

A Lesson in Thorns

Feast of Sparks

Harvest of Sighs

Door of Bruises

Misadventures:

Misadventures with a Professor

Misadventures of a Curvy Girl

Misadventures in Blue

The New Camelot Trilogy:

American Queen

American Prince

American King

The Moon (Merlin's Novella)

American Squire (A Thornchapel and New Camelot Crossover)

High Spice Historicals:

The Markham Hall Series

The Awakening of Ivy Leavold

The Education of Ivy Leavold

The Punishment of Ivy Leavold

The London Lovers

The Seduction of Molly O'Flaherty

The Wedding of Molly O'Flaherty

Far Hope Stories

The Chasing of Eleanor Vane

The Last Crimes of Peregrine Hind

The Conquering of Tate the Pious

Co-Written with Laurelin Paige

Porn Star

Hot Cop

About the Author

Sierra Simone is a USA Today bestselling former librarian who spent too much time reading romance novels at the information desk. She lives with her husband and family in Kansas City.

Sign up for her newsletter to be notified of releases, books going on sale, events, and other news!

www.thesierrasimone.com
thesierrasimone@gmail.com

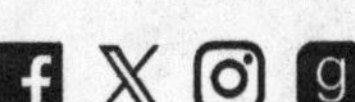   

www.ingramcontent.com/pod-product-compliance
Lightning Source LLC
Chambersburg PA
CBHW010558170726
48285CB00011B/2962